I0734055

Cindy M. Amos

SALVAGING

DOCTOR JUNK

By Cindy M. Amos

Hemmed in, yes;

I stood surrounded by the ill-intended.

They swarmed about me ready to harm.

Though on a cliff-ledge on the verge of falling,

God grabbed me and held me tight.

Psalm 118:10-13

Cindy M. Amos

ISBN-13:978-1-946939-08-1

Dedicated to my sister-in-law Sharon J. Amos

Who feeds the birds with a generous hand

each morning

and lives tenderhearted to all creatures,

great and small.

The author would like to acknowledge the following for their support and encouragement with this book:
istock for cover photo of Buffalo National River
Pamela Bower, Proofreader
Janice Fairbairn, Marketing Strategist for Series
Members of South Central Kansas ACFW Chapter
Cynthia Hickey of Forget Me Not Romances
& Inspiration of the Holy Spirit

LANDSCAPES OF MERCY SERIES
BOOK SIX

Yet there is one ray of hope:
God's compassion never ends.
Only the Lord's mercies have kept us
from complete destruction.
Great is His faithfulness;
His lovingkindness renews each day.

Chapter 1

*G**et the puppy and go.* Delayne Davidson tamped her sweaty palms against the steering wheel to seal her mission. She'd moved to the Ozarks at the start of April for her avian research, not to co-mingle with the natives. The car crept up a lengthy double rut driveway until a rabbit hutch-like shack came into view. So this was life in Ponca, Arkansas, the land that begat the headwaters of the gorgeous Buffalo National River.

Once parked, she opened the car door and heard elevated voices from the rear paddock. Lacking a fence, three shaggy goats roamed the yard near an old ringer washer, its tub overtaken by weeds. She headed toward the voices and gave her pocket a light pat to insure the puppy payment could be offered with ease.

An add-on feature snagged her attention up a giant blackjack oak tree. Beyond jumping height, the rim of a peach basket had been nailed into the bark. In an era where NBA teams played the sport in domed state-of-the-art arenas, little of that commerce had leaked into these Ozark backwoods. Money rarely circulated here, which left Newton County the second poorest in the nation. But she lived here now, so maybe she could be good for the local economy.

She shoved her hand into her pocket about the time a horse veered around the back corner of the house advancing at a gallop. Its hooves pounded the bare dirt yard. Two hands pulled at the horse's mane and, with some struggle, the torso of a man appeared.

After an instantaneous read on the wide-eyed panic, it became clear that no one had control of the situation. The horse snorted and inexplicably planted its two front hooves. The sudden stop then morphed into a sidestep maneuver. Having made a helpless cry, the rider cleared the horse's shoulders by a long shot. He soon hung upside-down off the flank closest to her.

Startled into action, Delayne sprang into a trot diagonal to the horse's new path. In seconds, the gray gelding would pass her like a good intention not acted upon. From out of nowhere, her uncle's old saying came to mind—to out-shy a horse you first have to out-sly a horse. Only an act of crazy would reel in this promenade. She dashed right for the horse, pulled the bills from her pocket, and aimed a strike at the branch directly over the horse's head. On impact, the wad of dollars separated and fluttered down like confused confetti.

Avoidance ruled. The horse tried to sidestep with all four feet at the same time. That move unlatched its rider and the man began to fall. His head struck against a sawed-off tree stump on the way down. When the dust settled, the horse stood stock-still, pulling several long breaths through its flared nostrils.

In direct comparison, the rider showed a lot less spirit. One hand moved up toward his head in slow motion, a damage control effort. Just short of making contact, his whole frame shuddered and the hand fell limp in the dirt.

"Lord, help me," Delayne muttered. With an eye on the wild steed, she made her way to the victim and knelt beside him. Her stomach flipped when she spotted the blood seeping from a gash over the man's left ear. His well-cropped hair had offered no padding for the blow, so the tree stump had gotten the better end of the deal. She pulled off the scarf from around her neck to apply pressure over the wound as footsteps approached behind her.

"Good one there, lady," a man said. "I never saw that trick before—throwing money to un-craze a horse."

Delayne turned to see a muscular young man in faded jeans begin to collect the wayward currency. She folded the scarf double and pressed it over the victim's ear with assertive force. When he winced at the contact, relief flooded over her. At least he was conscious.

An older woman dressed in a ratty pink housecoat and slippers wandered up beside the young man. In her arms, she held two wiggly Dalmatian puppies. "Make sure you get every last dollar, Tommy Lee. You know, for a new animal doctor, this tall fella don't know too much about horses. I could hardly get the words out edgewise afore he'd gone and bent Archie's ear back. He don't like that—not at all."

"Ma'am, I saw your sales flier and came out for a puppy." Delayne wished she could stand to address the owner eye-to-eye, but with the blood flow unstaunched, she had to stay put. "I'm glad to see you have a couple left. I'm here to buy one."

"Well, I already got her money," Tommy Lee replied. He fanned the hastily stacked bills for proof. "Go ahead and pick your dog." He gave a roguish smile and pocketed the cash.

The woman's face pinched. "Only this one here's available—the one with his cheek sewn up. Got a nasty gash from a nail poking out inside the doghouse. The vet here fixed it up good as new." She lowered the pup into a fold of the scarf.

The puppy scrambled to its feet and plunged its rounded belly against Delayne's arm. Happy for its freedom, its tail began to thump against the downed man's face.

He moaned and rolled onto one shoulder, facing her. "Stop the stampede, could you?" He exhaled and his eyes blinked open. Irises the color of rich amber flashed between his lids.

Delayne applied more pressure and freed one hand to guide the puppy to less injured territory. Her gaze skimmed the victim's face in time to catch the most amazing honey-brown eyes looking back at her. In an instant, they fluttered closed under lashes so long they could have swept her downriver.

"Guess you'll have to take him back to town," the woman said. "Our truck is near-bout out of gas. Tommy Lee can bring the doc his car come Monday."

Delayne started to protest, but the puppy licked her wrist as though to seal the deal. Somehow "get the puppy and go" had taken on some major baggage. She sighed and leveled her shoulders to lift the animal doctor. "Tommy Lee, you get his legs for me."

"Okay," he replied. "Let Maw hold your puppy. You've got your hands full of wrecked ve-ter-in-a-ri-an." The local-yokel managed to chop up the six syllables like making coleslaw out of the term.

His mother cackled as she caught the pup by the scruff of the neck. "Let me get the car door open. Front seat or back?"

Delayne stooped and slid her hands under the wounded man's arms. "Front, I think. I may have to hold pressure on his gash the whole way back to Harrison."

"Heavens, no," the victim sputtered.

Tommy Lee jerked his legs off the ground with a humorous smirk on his face. "Why, it sounds like Doctor Junk here don't appreciate your special treatment today. Maybe he's too messed up in the head to know pretty women are scarce around these parts." The man's smirk crept into a wicked grin.

In the moment, Delayne could only take comfort in the considerable height of the fallen man that now separated her from the fresh young flirt at his south end. At least the veterinarian, a man of advanced education accompanied with yet-to-be-determined social skills, would be the one coming with her—and the new puppy. Her next few steps came easier, and soon they had him loaded in the car.

The frazzled-haired woman closed the car door and handed her the scar-faced puppy. She stroked the remaining pup's head while trailing her around the front grill. "He'll need stitching up, he will. The walk-in clinic's your best bet at this hour. Sure wish Doctor Junk could have gotten something on old Archie's split hoof afore things went bad betwixt them."

Delayne brought the puppy into the car and lowered it with care into a box in the rear floorboard. A remedy for the doctor's unfinished work came to mind. She pressed the glove compartment open and withdrew a tube of Udder Butter cream. "Here, use this on the split hoof every night and keep him in a clean, dry stall. The split should clear up within a week. Goodbye now, and thanks for the puppy."

She started the car and shifted into reverse without glancing up. Once she exited the driveway, she noticed a tiny compact car parked along the roadside gully. A motion caught her attention and she checked her side-view mirror in time to see Tommy Lee give a friendly wave to send her on her way.

When the car dipped into a pothole down the road, her patient groaned and shifted against the seat. In the soft light of late afternoon, she got a close-up look at his chiseled features. Beyond notice until now, she spotted a well-trimmed chinstrap beard trailing along his jawline. She raised a hand to reapply pressure on the wound and, in a perk of placement, the tip of her middle finger fell atop the slender beard line. A combination of medical application and facial caress kept her occupied as the road curved back to town. Somewhere along the way, the squirmy puppy settled in for a nap.

"Well, well. Look what thirty-five dollars thrown into the Ponca wind can buy a girl these days—a speckled dog and a heckled doc." Amused at her predicament, she laughed and caught a glimpse of her newfound merriment in the rearview mirror.

"No respect," the passenger replied. A faint grin flitted across his face.

Piqued by the catty exchange, she dared to trace the beard line around the tip of his chin. Satiny under her fingertips, the contact sent a cozy tingle up her arm to her chest. *Mercy me.* She had to clear her throat to keep the conversation going. "Well, my daddy always told me a person receives the exact level of respect that they earn. Does that sit like a cap on today's animal-handling lesson?"

His long lashes twitched and his eyes fluttered open. "A dunce cap maybe. Large animal care will be the death of me yet. At least keep the speckled dog."

Delayne smiled at his reception of her teasing jab. "Oh, believe me, I plan to. I paid good money for this dog…good horse-shying money." She tapped her fingers on his chin and his next moan seemed to have less pain attached. The lights of town flickered around the curve as her rescue mission gained the unexpected sensation of hopeful promise.

Chapter 2

Kemp Junkowski ducked the tent flap and entered his outdoor classroom. With walk-in business more like creep-in at the animal clinic, he'd jumped at the chance to earn rent money by leading this training session for the park service. No stranger to emergency medical treatment, he had bartered for the add-on of wildlife rescue and rehabilitation. That would keep the shine on the DVM credential that followed his name on the clinic's door. Recouping the cost of that education had brought him to the doorpost of the Ozarks in the first place.

He spied a small table up front that held the device he would teach about in the opening session, an Automatic External Defibrillator. Drawn to it, he tossed a quick wave at a heavyset park employee in the first row and strolled over to examine the AED. When he recognized the familiar model, the tension in his chest loosened. He decided to forestall the shock of opening the storage cabinet housing the unit, so he could start his presentation with a rousing bang later.

The tent filled with seasonal employees as two uniformed men walked up from the back. With arms crossed and faces taut, the natural resources management staffers seemed to be escorting seriousness into the educational venue. They milled through the growing crowd as though hunting for something.

Kemp took a few seconds to remove small posters of the top five indigenous troublemakers in the vicinity for his second presentation. He aligned them on the table, no-touch-plants on the left and critters-to-avoid on the right. When the crease of a crisp-ironed sleeve brushed his forearm, he glanced up to recognize the individual who had hired him. "Good morning, Mr. Manning. Nice set of recruits you've hauled in today."

The division head spread his feet and regarded the defibrillator. "Mostly greenhorns in this lot, but they'll do. We're mixing morning training with afternoon fieldwork, so you get them at their most alert."

"Well, that's encouraging to know. I'm hoping they'll be able to recall these sessions if and when a more serious occasion rears its head." Kemp saw the flash of humor in the chief's eyes as his comment hit home.

The second man shook his head. "Don't count on total recall. I gave them a pop test on plant identification out in the field yesterday. The highest score came in at thirty, which I count as half an 'F.' Abysmal results."

"Doctor Junkowski, this is Ross Connors, our plant specialist," Manning said.

Kemp extended his hand and the botanist shook it as if his palm was full of poison ivy. "Guess you're focused on the spread of noxious weeds this summer."

"Among other blights, galls, and pestilences, yes."

Manning glanced at his watch and cleared his throat. "We'd better get started or we'll run into lunch break, the herd's favorite time of day. Hope you'll stay and eat with us, Dr. Junkowski. I think the chuck wagon is serving burritos today."

"Thanks, I'd be happy to."

Manning tapped a finger on his cheekbone. "Say, before I turn the group over to you, I need to make some morning announcements and take care of a little security housekeeping. We had an incident overnight in the department motor pool which I trust will not be repeated."

Kemp nodded and stepped aside as a foursome of loud recruits left the water station and filed to the back. When the muscular man turned, he recognized his client from Ponca—the one with the temperamental horse. He shifted his ball cap to finger the healing scar and stir the recollection. Angry heat seeped under his collar at the thought of unfinished business between them. The rube had returned his car to him—but not all of it.

Manning raised his arms to call for order while the plump recruit on the front row began to shush the mayhem quiet. "All right, let's get this session started. For those of you who can't remember or count days of the week after yesterday's scorcher, today is Thursday. Our focus today is human safety and wildlife savvy. The two are not always mutually exclusive when you're out in the field, so I suggest you stay alert for our guest presenter."

Kemp leaned back on the presentation table and

gave a thumbs-up at the mention. A motion at the edge of the tent caught his attention as a late-comer leaked into the group. Her light brown hair tousled and her jeans torn, the woman settled into the nearest available seat. When she turned to face the speaker, Kemp recognized his Ponca rescuer.

In short order, an entirely different reaction began to steam his collar. Not meaning to stare, he caught the wince when she flexed her knee where the tear resided in her jeans. He glimpsed scraped skin through the ripped fabric and eased over to his backpack where his obligatory first aid kit rode.

As the chief droned on about vehicle protocol, Kemp slipped behind him, circled the water cooler station, and approached the late-comer's chair. He offered the sanitizing wipe and adhesive bandage with a flick of his wrist. Why the flair of recognition in her eyes sparked the payback on his kind deed, he couldn't say. It sat on his skin like the shimmer of a bubble on his return trip up front, a real pulse-raiser.

Manning extended his palm in a truce. "Okay, enough policy and procedure. Let me introduce our presenter. Today we have Kemp Junkowski with us, the new veterinarian in Harrison. He comes by way of Chicago, so we're glad the windy city has blown him our direction. And, as you can see by his ready treatment of Delayne Davidson this morning, his medical expertise is not limited to the animal kingdom."

Laughter stirred beneath the tent's dome as Kemp assessed his audience. With their attention to the rescue device critical, he thought to shift the rear rows forward into better viewing range. When his gaze scanned by the female's seat, the two tabs of the bandage now rested on her thigh. Good. She'd fixed herself.

"Okay, Doc," Manning said in closing. "They're yours until eleven forty-five. Let the education begin."

Kemp strode to the front with a casual smile. "So—what do you do when the bottom drops out?" He let the rhetorical question hang in the air a few seconds.

A chortle sounded from the front row. "I usually run like heck in the other direction," the heavy-set recruit replied.

Kemp folded one arm across his chest and pointed at the young man with the other. "He's right, avoidance is a primary response. In the animal world, it's called a 'flee or fight' reaction. But humans are teachable—and that's where knowledge replaces fear. Today, we're going to deal with one of the most critical health situations that can land on anyone's watch—sudden cardiac arrest. And not since development of the CPR dummy have we possessed an aid like we have in this cabinet right here—an Automatic External Defibrillator, or AED."

Kemp flexed the palm of one hand open in front of the instrument. "Now join me in a moment of honesty. If you cannot see all five of my fingers at this instant, I want you to pick up your chair and move forward, making a semi-circle along the flanks here." He motioned in twin arcs around the sides of the table.

A ripple of movement started in the back and soon came accompanied by the sound of squeaking chairs. Nearly a fourth of his audience became swept up in the reconfiguration. Amid the chaos, Kemp's thoughts drifted through his presentation. He wished he could somehow alternate between showing and telling to make the demonstration more memorable.

The idea of a volunteer demonstrator popped to mind in a moment of enlightenment. He glanced around to assess candidates, skimmed past the chortling avoider on the front row until his gaze landed on a pair of rip-kneed jeans. Drawn to her, he had to make the perfect pitch for cooperation or he knew she'd balk at the request. Out of nowhere, the sensation of her fingering his beard during his accident flashed to mind. He bent toward her with a cozy smile. "Miss Davidson, I trust that knee is feeling better."

Her eyes crinkled at the corners. "Why yes, Doctor Junkowski, and I trust that head is feeling better."

Kemp touched the left side of his cap and nodded. His next move fell nothing short of baiting a hook. He slid his index finger down the narrow band of his beard from his sideburn to the tip of his chin.

The candidate sat transfixed, her eyes locked on his.

"I'm looking for an untrained volunteer to experience the stages of implementing the device firsthand as I narrate the proper procedure. Would you be so kind as to join me up front to fill that role?"

She played with a loose strand of sun-lightened hair and tucked it behind her ear. "I've already had my challenge of the morning."

"Good, then you're more alert than the majority of participants here. Come on, be a good sport and help me teach this in an interactive way they won't readily forget." He slipped just enough beg into his tone to sound vulnerable.

She tilted her face skyward and squeezed her eyes closed. "Oh, all right. Get me up there where you want me." She stood and winced.

"Here, lean on me. Your knee has tightened up." He offered his elbow and grabbed her chair with the other hand. "Was it much of a fall?"

She took his elbow and hobbled two steps. "A twenty-foot rock ledge on my survey route at daybreak."

He guided her toward the table. "Survey route?"

"I'm here to survey the ruffed grouse population in the park after a thirty-year reintroduction effort. It's been a notable success for the National Park Service."

He pulled her to a halt and positioned her chair off-center of the device. "You mean—despite an errant rock ledge here or there." This time he allowed the smile to shine through his eyes with a private gleam of gratitude that seemed to more than placate his volunteer. Her hazel gaze added to a few additional attributes as she took her seat in one ginger motion. He'd made the perfect selection for the up-close work. Now, he could let the heart attack begin.

Chapter 3

Never ask what's next. Delayne touched the front of the cabinet and the glass seemed cool. Maybe the temperature difference would translate up her arm, as she felt pretty heated and all too visible. Hopefully, they could get this done in a few minutes and take her off the hotplate.

The presenter bent toward her. "Hold up on opening the AED cabinet until I cue you," he whispered. A slight wink eclipsed one eye as he stood to face his audience.

His proximity somehow took the angular edge off of being up front. Delayne rested her hands on the tabletop and took a deep breath. She couldn't remember ever meeting anyone with amber-colored eyes. She'd have to ask him about his heritage if they got a minute alone. She looked past him and caught sight of Tommy Lee, the dog seller from Ponca, over on the far side. That's one heritage she wouldn't need to trace, due to extreme lack of interest.

Kemp strolled closer to the front row. "Distractions aside, I want you absolutely focused on what you're about to see and experience. Heart attacks are the number one cause of deaths in America. Environmental factors such as stress, heat, and overexertion can land a heart attack right in front of you. All the main facilities at middle and lower river here in Buffalo National River have these AEDs mounted in the lobby. Make it your job to note the exact locations the next time you visit these buildings."

Delayne snapped to heightened attention when he turned and paced toward her. Several chairs clunked together and a murmur started along one flank. Warm from the midday sun, she began to fumble with the top two buttons of her outer shirt.

Kemp stopped short of her station and quirked a smile aimed right at her. "I see Miss Davidson is getting comfortable in her role as primary rescuer. I want to thank her for her cooperation."

Someone stood in the far flank and began to make his way forward. "Hey, it looks like you might need a volunteer to play the dead man—and that's me."

"Not Tommy Lee," she whispered. When Kemp's gaze darted her way, she shook her head in deft refusal. She slung off the shirt and bared her shoulders to the task at hand.

Kemp shot up a stiff arm to halt the overzealous volunteer. "No thanks, Tommy Lee. I've already got the dead man covered. What I need is one more chair."

The heavy-set intern on the front row stood and offered his seat.

Kemp snapped his fingers at him and beckoned him

forward. "Why don't you stay up here as a sidekick, in case Miss Davidson needs a hand?"

An unstoppable flutter stirred the pit of Delayne's stomach as she embraced the inevitability of the demonstration. She swallowed and promised herself not to turn the lesson into a mawkish carnival show of medical ineptness. Before she realized it, Kemp had leaned closer to gain her attention.

"I'm your heart attack victim, but I may need to break character to emphasize a point to the class between steps on the AED. I hope that works for you."

Her heart squeezed in her chest. She managed a nod, though his direct gaze had sent a molten flow down her midsection. She'd never be able to keep any clinical distance between them at this rate. Desperate for some sort of compromise, she thought of a partial escape. "Okay, commentary intrusions are allowed— but you have to keep your eyes closed, or this isn't going to work for me." She squinted to narrow the field of negotiation.

Kemp straightened to his full height, his expression quizzical. The sidekick arrived and handed him the chair. "Fine. Dead man eyes as requested by Delayne here. And what's your name, sir?"

The recruit sucked in his gut to neaten his shirttail. "My name's Tim, but my friends all call me Timber. You know the saying, 'the bigger they are…'"

"All right, Timber," Kemp said. "Your job is to assist at any time an extra set of hands becomes an asset, otherwise, Delayne has the lead. I want you to remain posted off her shoulder. Now, give me a second to get my dead man chairs aligned."

Again, he caught her off guard with a direct stare.

She blanched under the close inspection and finally held up her palms as though she had nothing to hide.

"Your chair, Delayne. I need your chair. I doubt you'd be seated in a real-life situation, anyway." Kemp turned to face the audience. "For visibility purposes, I'll be laid out across these chairs, but you'd likely be working off the floor—or the ground—if the situation ever falls your way."

She rose and surrendered her chair to the instructor. Before she could release her hand, Kemp's warm palm clamped over it. The entrapment of his honeyed gaze caused her breathing to falter.

"You have to trust my words, okay?"

She busied her free hand with corralling a loose hair tendril. Her gaze met his and the rest blurred to background. Renewed confidence seemed to transfer from his hand. "I will."

"Great. Now don't let the machine rattle you when it gives the voice prompts."

Timber leaned a shoulder between them. "I'll keep her on the right path. Don't worry, Doc."

"We're set then," he replied with a tiny wink. He turned to the class and held his hands up for their attention. Soon, only the cicadas conversed beyond the tent. "For the next few minutes, it is imperative that you remember everything you see and hear. Got it?" He wiggled his fingers to prompt their response.

Delayne eyed the all-business medical cabinet in front of her on the table. "Help me, God," she muttered as a collective response of compliance rumbled back from the outer rim.

Within seconds, Kemp clutched his chest with a loud moan. He doubled over and cast himself across the chairs, face-up with his eyes squeezed closed.

"Quick, check the patient," Timber said as he nudged her with an elbow.

Delayne dropped beside him, squelched her knee pain, and began the basic ABC's of preliminary medical assessment. When she rose, it struck her to narrate her actions for the class's benefit. "I checked his breathing, which grew light to shallow. I also had a hard time detecting a pulse. Since I'm not sure at this point if it's a heart attack, I'm going ahead with using the AED."

Kemp raised his hand to draw their attention, but—to his credit—didn't open his eyes. "If ever at the crossroads of doubt, go ahead and deploy the AED. It will not allow you to deliver a shock erroneously, so the patient is protected if he or she does not require resuscitation." His hand dropped back down to dying position with a plop.

Delayne took that as her cue to open the cabinet. As Timber inched closer, she took a second to enjoy the confidence of a cool demeanor. She'd get this demonstration over with one-two-three and go back to her solitary existence as a birdwatcher in no time. "I'm opening the cabinet to gain access to the device now."

Her fingers fumbled with the latch, but conquered the mechanism in short order. When she guided the lid open, a screeching alarm sounded without warning. Her heart jumped in her throat, and her cool demeanor fell off the far edge of mayhem.

Timber threw his hands in the air. "Of course it has an alarm," he reasoned above the ruckus. "That alerts staff to any attempts at tampering with the box, right?"

Kemp raised his hand and flashed the okay signal to

confirm. The second the alarm quit, his hand sank into a lifeless role once again.

Delayne studied the oversized print on the instructions for operation. "I need to depress the start button to activate the machine. It's in the top corner here." She pressed down, overemphasizing the action for demonstration purposes.

A mechanical click awakened the device. "Secure the patient in a prone position and remove any obstructions to the chest region," it prompted with choppy enunciation.

She turned and knelt by Kemp. "Okay, I have to prep the patient for application of the device."

Timber stood over them which seemed to lower the dome of the tent. "His shirt's gotta go. Get with it."

Her fingers began a focused tumble down the cotton shirt's placard. To block Kemp's face out of immediate view, she shifted her shoulder forward, but not before she detected a slight crook denting his dead-man lips. *Mercy me.* Her patient seemed to be enjoying the tactile attention. A fluttered response tried to break free in her chest, but she had to stiffen her core and complete the unbuttoning job with her jaw clamped tight.

"Looks like we're ready to move on," Timber said.

"Yes, press 'next' on the machine," she replied.

His thumb struck the button. Dead silence leaked for protracted seconds.

The machine clicked with the cue. "Prepare the shock pads as follows. First, peel the one-time use adhesive pads from their protective coverings."

"This is my assist," Timber said. He grabbed for the plastic-wrapped pads and made quick work of freeing one.

Delayne reached to prompt the machine for the next step, but it made a noise, so she held off for a few seconds.

"Adhere a single replacement pad to the flat surface of the shock paddle. Then peel and adhere the free surface to the left side of the patient's chest. Be sure the surface contact is clear of any body hair. Shave if necessary."

She lifted the first paddle which remained tethered to the device by a thin wire. "Okay, there are two shock paddles here. I'm taking this first one."

"Here's the adhesive pad for it," Timber added.

"So now I stick this one-time use pad onto it and secure the connection to the patient's chest." She ran her palm to clear the skin surface with her left hand.

The patient's chin tipped down, revealing a slight grin. "My left, not yours," Kemp whispered.

"Rookie mistake," she exclaimed out loud. "Aim for the patient's left side, not your own. Think mirror image. Also, I need to comment that his chest is smooth, not hairy, so we didn't have to clear a surface for the pad." She eased the shock paddle into place and noticed his olive skin tone for the first time. A likely link with his amber eyes, she'd save that genetics small talk for another time.

The crinkle of wax paper drew her focus back as Timber handed her the second paddle. In seconds, she affixed it opposite its twin and rose to get adequate space between her and the patient. Despite his deadpan demeanor, the instructor seemed to gain allure as the situation grew tense, a game she wasn't ready to play. "Hit the button, Timber."

Her assistant poked a knuckle onto the switch and an electric hum responded. The sound of energy revving up to a hefty charge worked against the silence under the tent.

"I believe this is where the idiot-proof part of the device rears its decision-making head," she said to the class. Though she'd intended to sound more confident, the quiver in her voice failed to contribute to that impression.

"If not, this is going to be one heck of a reminder not to use a live volunteer," Timber added in a joking tone. The machine continued to surge, the whir increasing in volume.

The dead man raised his hand to interject an instructional point. "Remember, the main mistake you can make is to leave the AED device unused. All else is gain."

Within seconds, the whirring noise ceased. A metallic click followed. "This patient does not require defibrillation. Detach paddles and return apparatus to stored position."

Relief burst over Delayne like a water balloon smacking its target. Now she only had to disconnect the device and free the instructor to resume his lead.

"Okay folks. Break it up. No dead man here today," Timber teased. He twirled his dimpled wrist to demand feedback and got several laughs from the audience.

Delayne squatted beside Kemp and slid her thumbnail under one of the adhesive pads. "Time to get you out of this, Doc." The bond held tight, so she increased her prying pressure.

Kemp's hand flew up and clamped around her wrist. "Gentleness is a gift only the giver can bestow, Miss Davidson. As with a gaping head wound, moderate pressure will do."

The sting of his correction seared the end of the experience as she proceeded with the paddle detachment under suppressed enthusiasm. Soon, two red spots on his olive skin came as payback enough. Ever present, Timber took the used pads from her and headed to the trashcan.

A bit steamed that he'd felt the need to tweak her bedside manner, Delayne decided to leave the rest of the clean-up to Kemp. After all, she'd done justice to the assignment and the machine hadn't killed him. *What more could he ask for?* She dusted off her palms from further responsibility and straightened to face the audience.

"Here he is, class," she said with a smile. "You can have your alive-and-kicking instructor back now." She made a gracious sweeping gesture over the prone man. Unfortunately, he'd just risen to a seated position, so her animated backhand struck him in the solar plexus.

Kemp grunted and fell back over for effect. The unruly class members roared and began to applaud as the medical lesson defaulted to melodrama.

Ever the snubbed heroine, Delayne stuck her nose in the air and stomped off to the water cooler. She really needed a drink about now, in a gallon-sized cup.

"Ten minute break," Kemp called behind her.

While contemplating an early exit, she took a sip of the ice cold water and let it deliver its restoring power. Maybe she should stay. Wildlife was her primary interest, not being a medic.

The next person in line nudged her lightly. "You can still charge my chest anytime you want," Tommy Lee said. The leering gleam in his eye confirmed his sincerity.

"Keep your shirt on, Romeo," Timber replied. His plump arm soon pried an extra degree of separation between them. "Good job up there, Delayne. Doctor Junk sure picked the right volunteer."

"Primarily when he selected you, Timber. Let's partner together someday during training, maybe at controlled burning next week." She flashed him a smile to let him know she meant it.

Kemp appeared on the far side of the water cooler. "I've heard of a hostile witness before, but never a hostile volunteer." He passed his palm over his chest to make his meaning more than clear.

A tingle of embarrassment started to flush hot on her neck, so she decided to counteract it. "Here, let me cut back in line and get you some ice water for that accidental injury, doctor."

"Sounds fair."

She separated a cup out of the stack as Timber cleared the next recruit to open the tap for her. Distracted under the instructor's gaze, she got the cup off-center and the water dribbled down her jeans. Soon, the fire that had creased her knee all morning sizzled with momentary relief. She held the cup toward him and got the reward she wanted, amber forgiveness with an underlay of sweeping lashes. "Say, I've decided to hang around for the second session. Here's hoping your wildlife savvy is spot-on."

"Don't you know it," he replied. After rising in a toast for her challenge, the cup eclipsed every facial feature but his eyes. They seemed content right where they were focused—on her.

Satisfied, Delayne turned for her chair with the hope of regaining her post on the front row. It would prove to be an interesting morning, if only her knee would cooperate and bend a little.

27

Chapter 4

Saturdays spent on the Buffalo River might salvage his wasted weekdays in the clinic waiting for clients to walk in with their pets. Kemp studied the dark-streaked rock formation up ahead and understood the reason for the bend shown on his float map. The lure of the milky turquoise flow kept him focused on the river's next move. At one spot when he'd lost sight of the bottom, he spied a soft-shell turtle hunting minnows in the river rock below and gained his herpeto-fauna fix for the day. Lighthearted for the first time all week, he began to whistle.

On his right, the riverbank leveled into a grassy meadow that swept the landscape with wildflowers. A ranch house with a stunning rock façade anchored the property, a stone fence wrapping its flanks. Intrigued, he sank the tip of his paddle in the flowing waters and slowed the canoe.

A feminine figure moved around the far end of the stone fence and began to run toward the river. Her zigzag momentum crossed the meadow, which seemed to be a phantom chase with the morning breeze.

Amused, he steered into an eddy pool up ahead in hopes of viewing some grand finale as she ran out of real estate.

"No, boy, no," she called in a commanding tone. "Stop right there. No you don't. I just gave you a bath." She made a sweeping grab for something at her shoe tops and came up empty.

Kemp muffled his humorous reaction to her situation. The blondish wisps escaping her ponytail seemed familiar, but before he could settle on the recollection, a speckled belly with four sprawling legs appeared. With too much momentum to stop, the critter went airborne over the section of river he'd just navigated. The eddy helped him double back toward the impending splash. As memorable entries went, it did not disappoint.

The puppy bobbed to the surface with a waterlogged yelp. Kemp managed to slide his paddle tip under its belly and maneuver it toward his boat. Frantic to avoid rescue, the pup struggled against the prod and dunked into the mint-green waters again. A gasp shot down the bank behind him, but he kept his focus and soon saved the escapee by the scruff of its neck.

"Oh, what a relief. Thank you so much," the woman said. "Hold onto him and I'll be right down."

Kemp used a steering stroke to turn the canoe around. The Dalmatian shook its ears which sent a cascading tremble down its body to the tip of its tail. A love ambush followed when the puppy climbed his legs and braced against his chest in an attempt to lick his face. At such close range, he recognized the stitch job on the canine's cheek.

No longer needing to turn around to identify the pursuing female, he followed through because he wanted to. Back to him, she climbed down the stone steps that disappeared into the river. Clad in cut-off shorts that revealed curvy calves and a length of toned legs, her beauty began to steal the water's gemstone lure. The Dalmatian wiggled from his grip, its tail wagging. "Hey there, Delayne. I didn't know you lived around here."

She raised her sunglasses into her hairline as her expression vaulted through a series of reaction from recognition to something short of put-off, but her face soon warmed at the sight of her drenched pooch. "Hi, Kemp. I'm glad you happened to be on the river this morning, since my speckled demon decided to go AWOL."

"So you live on the upper river? That's pretty posh accommodations." He gestured to the rock house with his paddle handle.

"It's park service housing. They acquired the private property to protect the watershed. This used to be an Arabian horse ranch called Lost Creek."

"Aha, eminent domain—another form of hostile volunteering." When he related the two, she squinted as though he'd touched on a sore spot. "Hey, you're not still holding that pressure comment against me, are you?"

She shifted her sunglasses down like a tinted shield. "Well, I thought I'd done more than you'd asked at the AED training session, so yeah, the criticism stung a bit."

"That wasn't my intention at all. I apologize. When I see an effort teeter on the edge of perfection, I offer advice to get it there, that's all. I even had to be schooled on proper pressure myself, once upon a vet school dreary. Forgive me, will you?" The puppy sank its dagger-sharp teeth through the toe of his water shoe. He released the paddle and captured it in both hands.

"See, I told you—a speckled demon." She struggled with a laugh, but finally allowed it to win out over a less sunny disposition. "Okay, you have your forgiveness, Doctor Junk. And thanks for your impromptu rescue by fishing Strappy out. He must think he's part Labrador."

"Strappy, huh? Does that have anything to do with his scar-line looking like a beard?" The puppy thrashed to get free, so he pinned it against his chest which earned him a chin cleaning.

"Maybe. Hey, you did a great job on the cheek repair work, so thank you. After your stall-side manner with the horse up in Ponca, I had some initial doubts."

"I appreciate your commendation. That means there's hope for me yet, I guess." Though he smiled, the moment seemed stilted with him afloat and her flat-footed on the slab. Something had to give. The eddy soon swirled the boat until she came within reach. He could hand over the pup and end the chance encounter, but another idea held much more potential. "Say, if you're not doing anything special this morning, how about coming on a float with me? My car's waiting at the Pruitt take-out, and it's only a band of turquoise water between here and there. No strings attached, just pure recreation."

"Really? I'm not doing anything special today—and

I've be dying to get out on the river. If I say yes, are you going to make me dog-dive to land in your boat?" She peeked over her dark lenses and gave a teasing grin.

Thrilled to have her company, he looked for a way to maneuver the boat. "Great. I think I can align with your landing—if Chinstrap here will let me." He reached for the paddle and the puppy nipped at his knuckles.

She snapped her fingers. "Okay, give me a few seconds. I just remembered the paddle I found down here last week. Let me run back up the steps and grab it." She climbed several steps and glanced back at him. "Do you have drinking water?"

"Plenty, plus an apple and a granola bar that I'll arm wrestle you for later." The inference of contact heightened the slight buzz of anticipation.

Delayne reached the top step and hoisted an old wooden paddle over her head. "Now disembarking to Pruitt—and that granola bar you mentioned is going to be mine." She descended with grace to realign with the river.

Kemp took a lengthy stroke to glance the bow off the rock landing. In a quick maneuver that rocked the gunwales, he gained a passenger. Before he could face the boat downstream, the puppy had claimed its owner by the shoestring. "You should kick those sneakers off and lend the little cuss some entertainment."

"Great idea, Doc. Yes, I agree—there's some hope for you yet." She kicked free from her shoes and positioned her weight more centrally to take the first paddle stroke. Accentuated with a flourish of follow-through, it sent an extra splash back in his vicinity.

Buoyed by her companionship, he could hardly separate the lure of her hope-filled admission from the refreshing splash that came his way. Now, his nature study down the watercourse had a centerpiece that did a masterful job of attracting his attention. Or was that distracting his attention?

"Wow, this sun is intense for mid-May." She took a stroke and let her fingers skim the water. "Wish I had a hat."

"Sorry I can't loan you mine. I'm still protecting that gash on my head and have to hide it from Mr. Sun. Maybe I've got something in my float bag we could rig."

"No—I've got this, captain." Her paddle clunked against the fiberglass hull as her hands set about the hat-making venture.

Kemp used the transition to study the riverbank. He steered them under the towering rock bluff which seemed to dwarf the world into the strand of mint julep which kept them afloat. When her cotton shirt flew off her shoulders and wrapped her head like a mammy's kerchief, he tried not to notice the bright green athletic top now hugging her upper torso. Aversion wouldn't be an option forever, though, as he had to keep his eyes on the river.

"I've never seen this stretch before—even though it's right in my own front yard." She turned to face him as though to share the wonder of her revelation.

He chuckled at the row of knots that now served as a brim to shade her eyes. "I've never seen it either. It's beautiful—and drenched with color, too." His chest tightened, so he worked the sensation into a power stroke that propelled them along the rock face.

Delayne took a leisure stroke that flexed her shoulder muscles under the cross-strapped top. Her second stroke extended into a healthy splash. The puppy barked and lapped at the water that dripped from a brace. "That's for you guys in back—to keep the color drench going."

Kemp rested his paddle over his knees and shirked off his wet T-shirt. "Hey, two can play at that game." He draped the shirt over his water supply and decided to take a steering stroke to see if she'd like a closeup of the overhanging willow ahead. Once his paddle lifted from the water, it may have had some extra English on it, as it kicked a spray toward the bow.

She inched toward the tree with a giggle. "Hey this is fun. I can't believe I'm on the Buffalo River. Best day ever." She reached her paddle into the weeping fronds of the willow and blended with the scenery.

The connection between female and flora moved him for some odd reason. He let the scene play out until he could reach the same branch—which he did with tactile pleasure. "Not a bad outcome for a speckled, belly-flopped beginning. No, not bad at all."

She gave him a glimmer of attention over her shoulder. "I'm inviting you to my place for a late lunch afterwards, to thank you for asking me out on the river. I'd like to show off some of the ranch's hidden architectural wonders, so please say you will."

His satisfaction slipped into a gear higher than companionship, one with better attraction. "Lost Creek for lunch? It sounds like a destination right off my float map. Who'd want to miss out on something like that?" The puppy barked at the shoestring knot on its muzzle.

"Great. That settles it. Strappy gets his puppy kibble

and, for you, I'm cooking over the fire pit out back." She pushed off a menacing rock and the bow glided into open water.

Kemp assessed the scenic spot and decided to slow their voyage to prolong her close company. He lowered his frame into the hull and used his shirt to pad his back as he leaned against the stern seat. "This might be a good place to take a siesta. You guard the fort, Miss Davidson…and try to keep Yappy quiet."

"Are you serious? Okay, captain. Take forty winks if you must. I'll pull us through this stretch." She doused her paddle to prove it.

Kemp closed his eyes, his last focal point her optic green centerpiece. Between that and the gentle sway of the boat, he hit relaxation island in no time. Soon only partially aware, he heard the puppy drag the shoe across the center rib. No matter. The whole world soon turned tranquil in a sun-drenched dream where time stood still.

A pair of wet hands soon beat on his chest. He sat up, saw the river, and got his bearings.

"Kemp—there's a snake in the bow. Come fish him out before Strappy sees it." In hurry-up mode, Delayne offered her hand.

He crouched to his feet and accepted her help. He'd be happy to enjoy the snake a little before returning it to the river. When he tried to step around her, her arms locked around his waist. Suddenly, they were headed over the gunwale for a premeditated dunk.

"Swim time," she said with a teasing tone. Her guilty smile flashed in the sun.

His only protective move, he drew her tight against him for the splashdown while the puppy barked its protest at being the last one left on board.

~

Delayne surveyed the leftovers and thought her guest should have eaten more. "Maybe this sauce didn't work with the pork."

Kemp crossed his ankles and shook his head. "Nonsense, and the wood fire charred the flavor even deeper. You can't buy food that good at a restaurant. I ate plenty." He flexed his shoulders and stretched.

"Thanks. I hope you're not so sore you need to skip my tour. I wanted you to see the ranch. The original owners really put some work into this place." She pulled back her drying hair and snapped the band in place.

"Let's put the skewers away so Soggy won't get into it. I don't advocate table scraps for little guys like him, as he needs the nutrition in the dry puppy food."

"Yes, Doc. Give me a minute, and then we'll tour the grounds. Please don't wake up the puppy. I'm trying to keep him out of the barn area. It's pretty weed-infested, as the park service doesn't keep that part maintained."

He raised a finger to his lips in immediate cooperation and stood to help her collect the dinnerware. "I've never seen a patio like this before. So inviting, it draws you outside from every main room of the house."

"I typically frequent the eat-in kitchen and the back bedroom there. The park service could really use this place for an upper river retreat if they had any creativity. Why everything has to operate from mundane Harrison, I'll never understand." She lifted the skewers and led him in through the kitchen door.

"So that's where you're working? I think you're

only a block or two from my fledgling animal clinic. You should bring Scrappy in for his next round of shots sometime soon."

"I hardly think Mr. Manning would like a chewing machine in headquarters all day if I bring the dog to town."

"You could leave him with me. He can have the run of the clinic like a mascot. Maybe I need a dose of cute polka-dots around the place to help build some ambiance." He shrugged and left the dishes in the sink.

"If you can help me crate train him, I just might take you up on the offer."

"Be glad to. You don't need an appointment. The clinic opens daily at eight."

"Don't be surprised if you see us by Tuesday then." She pulled a length of plastic wrap out and snapped it around the leftovers. "Guess you don't have a pet of your own?"

"Not yet. I'm partial to reptiles and amphibians, but wanted to give myself the freedom to get the clinic up and running first. I'm living upstairs in a loft apartment. It's convenient, but nothing like this." He motioned toward the grand foyer.

After storing the food, she waggled her brow and crooked a finger over her shoulder. "Let's go out the back way. I want to start your tour at the stone well." Thinking to keep some distance between them, his weighty stares certainly held added gravity. When she stepped past the slumbering pup, she gave Kemp a finger-on-the-lips reminder. He didn't seem to mind the contact. The round well soon came into proximity and she stopped in front.

"No doubt at one point, the rancher drew water for

both his family and his livestock—all from right here." She bent into the mouth of the well to test if she could see the bottom. It reflected a round slice of late afternoon sky.

Kemp leaned in beside her. "This would be a long haul to the barn, wouldn't it?"

"Only no one's got to haul the first bucket of water. Take a look at this." She stepped around the well and on its lower side, a rock-lined trough stretched down the slope.

Kemp grinned. "This *is* a work of genius. Don't tell me it goes all the way to the barn."

"Find out for yourself. You can even walk the trough if you'd like. I prefer terra firma."

In full embrace of her challenge, he leapt into the stone-lined channel. He set an ambitious pace with his long legs as the conveyance wound around to the east end of the barn.

Delayne drank in his fluid motion. Confident while inquisitive, he struck her as the Eagle Scout type, a leader in his class and always prepared. She needed to get to know more about him.

"Hey, first one to the barn door gets to pick our next destination," Kemp said with a glance back.

"Oh sure, give yourself an advantage."

"Come on, slow poke. I'll halt and give you three seconds."

Even before he could get the words out, she shot past him in a burst of determined energy. She would have the say on their next destination, as he didn't know his way around these parts like she did. His footfall echoed close behind her right before the barn. Delayne lunged for the rough wood and touched the door panel a split second before her guest. "Home-court advantage," she puffed between breaths.

Kemp bent, short of air. "You didn't trust my pick, I can tell. This ranch is amazing, though. A water system that delivers itself—who'd of ever thought?"

"Ingenuity. Sometimes you can bottle it—or at least channel it downstream." When she smiled up at him, he didn't look away. "How about we stroll back to those stone steps on the river? I'd like to chat a bit about family heritage and faith."

He leaned on the barn door, enigmatic against the peeling paint. "Sure, beside the river sounds perfect. That's how I'll remember this day—a turquoise band of water with you set in the center of it. A more enlightened man might call that lovely on beautiful, if adequate words can be found."

Pulsed by his admission, she broke into a run for the river. Maybe she'd try to set the memory into something more lasting, or perhaps she'd slip in the aqua waters and take a late swim. All that mattered was that he followed. She turned back to make sure.

He came after her at a full run.

Chapter 5

Delayne crammed the latest issue of her survey map into the console and tried not to think about how early she had to get up in the morning. The ruffed grouse had resettled in the Ozarks with ease, so maybe they wouldn't mind her tapering off the survey frequency from every other day. Male birds would cease to drum for romantic business by month's end anyway, so she only had a couple more weeks to get her data logged.

She eased the car down Second Street on her way to pick up her speckled roommate. Its first day in doggy daycare, she hoped the experiment had been good for all parties involved. When her thoughts skittered to the tall vet, she leaned over and checked her hair in the mirror. It had the frantic thrown-together look of early bird nest.

She would have liked to pretend that looks didn't matter, but couldn't deny how flattering Kemp's lingering glances had become. Maybe she needed to try a little harder, as twenty-seven-year-old researchers didn't rate much in the male attention department. She moaned, dug a small brush out of the console, and parked one-handed as she tried to look presentable. "God, please help me cover the important stuff—and lend some grace with the rest. Amen."

Kemp exited the front door of the clinic with her pet carrier in one hand. He gave her a reserved wave and stepped down the curb. "Shhhh. Chinstrap's asleep."

She ducked to peek through the door's grate and saw a speckled mass of slumbering pup curled into its favorite blanket. The cozy scene tugged at her heart.

"One of us couldn't keep pace," he whispered with a wink. "Here's our full day. He played outside, made friends with a Doberman, and ate half a shoe. I still don't know where he found it—the shoe, I mean. The Doberman was an ear job, cosmetic but paying. That about sums up our day. How about yours?"

Her jaw dropped that he would even think to ask. "Oh, Ross Connors and I disagreed about the suitable plant cover on the remainder of my survey grounds. He drew up the route maps based on his assumptions, but I think increased elevation has limited the population on some peaks. At any rate, dawn will seem late tomorrow morning. I'll already be hitting the trail up an old logging road to count males on a documented drumming log."

His eyes sparkled. "That must be a thrill, getting a close, behind-the-scenes look at such a secretive species. I certainly envy your field work."

"But not my sleep deprivation, right?" She forced a quiet laugh and popped the rear door open so he could load the pet carrier.

When he exited, he stuffed his hands into his pockets. His gaze dropped to his toes.

She stepped away from the car, feeling a little trapped. "What? You need to tell me something, don't you?" The unease magnified as seconds ticked by. "Hey, if the puppy is a problem, you don't have to take it."

"No, the set-up's great. And I want to keep the training going. Plus, I kind of like the little cuss." He kicked the curb, but still wouldn't look at her.

"Okay then. There's something else you're not saying." A dread crept into her thoughts as the scene had all the makings of trouble. "Come on, Kemp. Just be honest."

He pulled his hands free only to lock them behind his neck. "It's like this. I need to go pick up some posters for a upcoming state-sponsored rabies clinic called 'Cures for Canines.' Anyway, the central distributor is located in Hot Springs. Would you like to ride up there with me one day after work?"

"That's it? You froze up like a totem pole just to ask me out?" She shot him a questioning look that may have come across a bit testy, given her argumentative day.

"You're right. I'm an absolute klutz at this type of thing. A client mentioned that Hot Springs was touristy and fun so I thought…well, never mind. Forget it." He raked his fingers through his hair, but winced upon contacting the healing scar above his ear.

Touched by his awkwardness, she stepped up the curb and reached for his wound, using care this time. Though his eyelashes flinched at the contact, she held her place. "You invited me, so now it's my responsibility to give you an answer. Yes, I'd like to go to Hot Springs with you." She smoothed his mussed hair and traced his beard down his jaw before letting go.

He worked through the momentary stun. "We'll be on the road late getting back, so I don't want to interfere with your early mornings. What day would work best for you?" He tilted his head as though asking for help.

"I can sleep in Saturday, so Friday night would be best for me." A complication flitted to mind. "What about Strappy?" She motioned toward the back seat.

"I think the pup has to play third wheel," he replied with a teasing tone. "We can't let it go all day without human interaction, now can we?"

"No, not for the best results, anyway." She inhaled and glanced down the street to gain perspective. "Thank you for giving me something to look forward to, Kemp. I have burn boss training Thursday near Pruitt, so we won't be coming back to town until Friday anyway. I'll drop Strappy by in the morning, if that's good with you."

"Sounds like a plan. Let's eat dinner in Hot Springs after I pick up the posters. Then we can tour around wherever we want to go." He rubbed his palms together, seeming more at ease.

"Fine. By the way, how did I do with the pressure application this time, Doctor Junkowski?" She stepped down to street level with a coy smile.

"Let's say it's working uphill from adequate. Who knows? Perhaps Friday night will find you in top form."

"Don't you wish?" She shook her head and slid into the driver's seat. In an accentuated reach for the seatbelt, she tried to cover her blush. When she looked up again, he stood leaning on the clinic's door, his honey-warm gaze fixed on her. She unclamped three fingers from the steering wheel and tossed him a little wave as she backed from the curb. *Mercy me.* She had a Friday night date.

~

It took Kemp until Wednesday night to have a first-class case of guilt for asking Delayne out. If the Doberman's owner hadn't paid in cash, he wouldn't have had a dime to his name. He was vested lock, stock, and barrel in the clinic. It needed furniture in the reception area, but he couldn't begin to afford it. The "Cures for Canines" event paid back pennies per shot, but at least it paid something. Maybe he could do a follow-up visit promotion and lure some future business that way. He had to build up the clinic so it could sustain itself—and a hungry veterinarian.

He cranked the manual can opener around the rim of a can of beans, his lucrative dinner. The lid dropped onto the mat-gray countertop and made at artistic improvement. Maybe he'd let it stay for awhile. He dumped the beans in a bowl and headed for the antique microwave. With a turn of the dial, he was cooking the evening's fare. Much ado about nothing—but at least his empty stomach would be satisfied.

His glance fell to the pile of mail he'd put off examining that afternoon in deference to cleaning the kennel area in back. Most of the letters were credit card applications or solicitations from local banks. A glossy postcard for a local caramel popcorn company caught his attention. He could model his advertisement after that. Seeing the address wasn't too far down the road, he thought to stop by and inquire as to who they had used for their color printing.

An image of Strappy curled up on his red blanket flashed to mind. The pup certainly would make a good-looking canine client to feature on the card. Delayne might be open to that. At this point, he needed all the free cooperation he could get.

When he reached for the platinum credit card application, he uncovered a hand-addressed envelope. Intrigued, he tossed the junk mail aside and picked up the card. Not only had the sender spelled his name right, they had also added the DVM behind it, a rarity. The microwave dinged, but he ignored it and tore open the flap.

Dear Doctor Junkowski,

When a man endeavors to care for the animal world, he has undertaken a noble intent. That is not to say it will be easy, but I assure you it can be highly rewarding. Should you need an empathetic listener, my clinic door is always open. I'm only forty miles to the north, as the cockatoo flies. Best wishes for your establishment in Harrison,

Doctor Gaylord of Eustace Springs Animal Clinic

Kemp dropped the note and headed for the microwave, driven by his hunger. Once he had the molten feast in hand, he doubled back to check the envelope. Yes, the sender had included a full return address. Not one to allow a fortuitous contact to fall by the wayside, a flurry of questions and concerns rushed to mind. Maybe a mentor was just what he needed. He grabbed a spoon and let his thoughts coalesce as he planned his letter of response. Perched at the dinette table, he remembered to give thanks for the meal—and the newfound supporter.

As the evening grew late, his surge of enthusiasm waned, but the letter had been written. Now, he only needed a stamp to send it on its way. He could close the clinic over lunch tomorrow and head for the post office. Picking up fast food remained out of the question, as he had to save every cent for Hot Springs. Delayne popped to mind, but instead of dreading the expense of the encounter, he could only think of her stimulating conversation and the way she often punctuated it with laughter. He stood to go brush his teeth and touched his scar, wondering if she would care to caress it again. A man could only hope for such an intangible wealth as good companionship. And he did.

~

Delayne blinked as the wind shifted out of the southeast. They'd been paired in burn crews all morning, learning suppression pointers and proper firefighting techniques that came with prescribed burns. The term "controlled burn" might have stretched the abilities of this crew. Ross Connors already had a conniption over lax safety along the fire line. She wouldn't want to see his reactivity escalate.

She tried to find Timber, but he'd hidden his bulk as the radio coordinator for the chief burn boss. Right now, that was Tommy Lee Resnick, which is why she chose to hang back. *Out of sight, out of mind.* At the very least, she could hope for smoke to hide behind.

A figure walked up from the tanker truck, a back-up precaution in case things got hotly out of hand. She turned to find Ross Connors headed her way. She took a drink from her water bottle and replaced the cap. Maybe they could get along today.

"Davidson, I need you to go relay the wind change to the burn boss. I can't seem to get the lead crew to respond by radio. That's a red flag for me, as continuous communication is essential. They shouldn't run the fire line up that next ridge under the wind shift, so go put a halt to the advance. Tell them I said to mop up where they've already been, and we'll break for lunch a half hour early." He crossed his arms and glared at her.

"Yes, sir. The wind is out of the southeast now. With the ground moisture drying up in the direct sun, there's too much fuel over on that ridge, I agree. Timber has our radio, but I'll go find them and make sure they don't extend the fire line." She turned and broke into a trot, but not before she heard his growl of disdain. Friendly or not, she would deliver the message and pull the greenhorns back before any harm could be done.

She diverted around a small stand of oaks that had managed to stay clear of the training. After passing a towering rock formation, she crossed into the wooded glen where the bulk of the training had taken place. White-gray smoke curled from the west flank, so she followed the signal to find the crew. Timber appeared first, bent and wheezing from too much exposure. "We're dropping back, partner," she said with a pat on his shoulder. "You go to the truck and let Connors know I found you guys. It's mop-up from now until lunch, so go breathe clean air."

"Do you want the radio, Delayne?" Timber unclipped the unit from his belt and waved it in front of her.

On impulse, she followed her usual preference to

travel light and declined possession with a shake of her head.

Timber shrugged and strode east out of the woodlands to carry out his duty.

Delayne assessed the crew's position and decided to make a diagonal cut to intercept them, the wind at her back. She ran across a burned area where several stumps still smoldered. They'd have to come back through here on mop-up and make sure to snuff out everything. Up ahead, she saw two seasonal staffers and raced toward them.

As she approached, she saw that they had too much fresh fire line going to make pulling back a simple affair. Leave it to Tommy Lee to ramp things into hyper-drive to make a show of his leadership skills. She cupped her hands to her mouth to exaggerate her yell. "Halt the fire. We've had a wind shift. Connors said to hold up, guys." Winded, she ran closer to make sure they'd heard the directive.

An intern with a rake held up his gloved hand and gave her the okay sign. He shouted something indiscernible to the bearer of the drip torch. Two other members dropped back off the line. One intern raised a radio to his face to communicate the change, just like they'd been trained. The smoke soon began to thin.

Relieved to have such immediate cooperation, Delayne scanned the area and determined they were far enough away from the next ridge to not risk losing control due to the wind shift. She approached the torch bearer only to discover it was Tommy Lee.

"I think we can torch that stand of saplings over there and finish cleaning this place up."

She wiped grit from her cheek. "No, Connors

commanded the crew to stand down due to the wind shift. I'm relaying his message. We're on mop-up from now until lunch, got it?"

"Mopping up is for sissies—and girl members of the crew. I'm the burn boss, so you're not telling me what to do, Miss By-the-book." His leer showed a flash of white teeth between two sooty lips.

"Give up the drip torch, Tommy Lee. I'll not let you endanger the crew."

"I'm going to give these woods a redneck whopping and nobody's going to stop me, leastwise you." He spat and hauled the torch closer to his intended target.

"Stop. You're being negligent, not redneck. There's a liability here for the park service. Think about that for a second. If that blaze goes over the ridge, we won't be able to suppress it."

"Don't panic when things get a little hot, Delayne. That makes you seem helpless." He relit the flame and let it rip a fiery arc between them.

"Fall back, guys. You're not responsible for this breach of command. Somebody go tell Connors we might have trouble with the amount of fire let out. Get the truck back here if you can manage it." When she turned to be sure they had understood, the interns were already running out of the woods. Now she stood alone against Tommy Lee and his linear fire. She needed a tool.

From where the crew had halted, she spotted a handle leaning against a tree and darted for it. To her instant dread, footsteps followed behind her at a run. Tommy Lee might be easily distracted from his burn boss duty, but she refused to be the bait. She lunged for the shovel, swung its handle over her shoulder, and struck the pursuer right on his helmet.

Dazed, he stumbled back but caught his balance. When he looked up at her, Tommy Lee looked like the devil incarnate—singed, red-faced, and hell-bent for evil. "You and fire might be a hot combination to my liking, Delayne."

"Let's just say you're never going to find out, Resnick." She stuck the handle lengthwise between them. "It's one thing to disobey orders, but hotter water to commit sexual assault. I'm warning you not to touch me, Tommy Lee. Don't even try it."

His laugh caught in his throat. He turned up the drip torch as though to outmaneuver her. It licked a blue flame between them.

She stood firm, scheming where to strike with the shovel. She opted for the side opposite the torch, so he couldn't use the canister to block the blow. Once he made his fiendish advance, she took a power-swing and made contact. As he fell, he hooked her with his elbow and they tumbled together, the flame tip grazing past her head too close for comfort. Before she knew it, Timber had jumped into the fray and used his bulk to squelch the misbehavior. On hands and knees, Delayne crawled away as other members of the crew came to lend some aid.

Connors glowered at her from the truck. "Women in the field…it always breeds trouble."

"You file the harassment report or I will," she replied. Before standing, she found her helmet and raised it to her head. A hunk of singed hair promptly came off in her hand. When she looked back at Connors, she found him squelching a smile. "Come on, guys, we've got a fire line to put out. Everybody get a tool and let the suppression truck take the lead."

Connors floored the accelerator and the truck circled east out of the smoke. Soon Timber appeared and tossed a shovel-full of dirt past her.

The heat of the previous encounter seemed to lessen with his presence. "So, what do you think of women with short hair, Timber?"

"Well, are they in the kitchen cooking or not?" He snickered and slid his upturned shovel over a licking flame to snuff it out.

"Looks like lunch may be a long way off now."

"Yeah. Tell me about it."

Delayne glanced at the dense vegetation along the upper ridge and knew that she'd saved it from certain destruction. Too bad she couldn't say the same for her own hair.

Chapter 6

Well after dusk, Kemp slowed the car as it hugged the banked curve on the road to Hot Springs. Shadows fell across Delayne's face from her tilted position in the passenger seat. He admired her attempt to keep the dog entertained one-handed in its crate on the back seat, mainly because she had to lean closer to him to achieve that contact. She'd talked non-stop for the first twenty minutes out of Harrison, which seemed somewhat out of character for her. With hours of solitary field time to compensate for, he let her rant.

"You know, at least Manning was decent enough to write down my claim. Evidently, Connors had no intention of filing any report. He was right there for part of the attack—an eyewitness. Do you know what he had the nerve to say to me?"

"No, what?"

"He said that women in the field were nothing but trouble. So that makes it my fault for provoking

Tommy Lee simply by being out there. Let's ignore the fact that I kept that zealous pyromaniac from burning down the next hillside. A 'blame the victim' mentality doesn't sit well with me." She slapped her palms together and white hairs went airborne. The puppy yelped at being abandoned. Delayne exhaled and looked ahead at the descending road. "Please let me bring him up front here, Kemp. I'm about to get a crick in my neck from turning around."

"No can do. Veterinarian's rule—the critters stay in back. At least my car isn't as big as yours, so you can reach. By the way, Tommy Lee has a strike against him in my book, too. I don't think I ever told you." He glanced at the on-coming car and clicked his bright lights off. Maybe if he changed the subject, she could calm down some.

"Never told me what? That his old gelding had cut its hoof, not worn a split in it?"

"Really? You could tell that? I never even got a close enough look."

"Yes, I'm reasonably sure. I left his mother some hand balm to put on it and told her to keep the horse in a clean stall. From the looks of that place, I doubt she could find one inch of clean space. I shudder to think what Strappy's doghouse must have looked like." When the pup yipped at his name, she stuck her hand back to give it another round of attention.

Kemp leaned toward her to close the gap, which wasn't far. "About my strike against Tommy Lee. You know he brought my car back to town that following Monday morning when he came to work, right?"

"Yeah, I think his mother promised something like that. I saw your car parked on the main road as I pulled out that day."

"Well, he did bring the car back—but not all of it." He let the mystery hang in the air between them and tried to focus on the road. When he managed a glimpse of her face profiled in the mirror, she looked duly perplexed.

"I see he didn't take out the back seat—such as it is." She started to giggle and tried to swipe it away with her non-doggy hand.

"Something is missing, so guess again." He'd get her out of this fired-up mood yet.

"Oh, I know. It's that wind-up crank thing that starts this squirrel cart. Right?" Her giggle came back and this time she let it run free.

"No, and I lost the smiley face ping-pong ball from my antenna before I moved down. So I already thought I was traveling light." He grinned and let his gaze flit to hers for an instant.

"Give me a hint. I can't come up with anything." She leaned so far toward the puppy that her chin made contact with his shoulder.

He raised one eyebrow to let her know the contact had registered. "Try thinking of something extra…something not visible, so you might not notice for awhile if it was gone."

"Oooh, invisible but extra. The air in your tires? Ha! Ha!"

He tried to hold his pleasure at bay with a smirk, but she inched even closer as though to pry the answer out of him with feminine charm. *Time to be obvious.* "You're so close, you could drop your tire iron on it."

"Your spare tire? That's it, isn't it?" She grabbed the cap of his shoulder and gave it several squeezes.

"That's it! Tommy Lee Resnick stole your spare and sold it for…for grocery money for his maw." She slapped her knee and belly-laughed.

This grew far too entertaining for a drab drive to pick up rabies literature. Kemp let the satisfaction of having Delayne with him seep deeper for a few seconds. He even blinked to make sure it was real. There she sat, right beside him smiling.

"Well, Kemp, that makes you a victim just like me. I guess I'll have to treat you special now, lest your victimization establish a pattern of downtrodden behavior from which you never recover. That's what they taught us to guard against in sociology class." She patted his shoulder sympathetically and must have thought better of it. In seconds, she planted a kiss on the padded part of his upper arm.

Flushed by her intimate contact, it didn't help matters that the dog had been making constant licking noises from the crate in back. His heart rate escalated. The car deviated from its lane. Soon the tires hit the rumble strip on the outer curve as a warning.

Delayne's hand touched his where it rested on the steering wheel. "Easy, tall guy."

"Tall guy, huh?"

"Yes, and I remember thanking God for all that height—as it put me further from Tommy Lee when we had to cart you off the premises in Ponca." Two dimples soon marked her humor.

"So glad I could oblige the lady, especially since I was none too cognitive at the time."

"I recall giving thanks that a man of some refinement and advanced learning happened to be the one trapped in the car with me, not the other possibility."

"Do you mean Maw Resnick?" He gave her a teasing look out of the corner of his eye.

Her hand landed on his shoulder. "No, Doctor DVM. I'm talking about Mister Big Flirt."

"Well, all things considered, Miss Davidson, I think you've made the right pick." He rubbed the edge of his chin across her fingers and saw her eyes smolder. Though he needed to keep his focus on the road, something more remained to be said. After all, he'd put her controlled burn rant out with a fire of his own. "Just for the record, I'm having a good time."

"Me too. Such good medicine—to get away." She straightened in the seat and let her head fall back. The contact freed several singed wisps of hair from her braid.

"Are you getting hungry?"

"Starved. How much longer?"

"Less than ten minutes. It won't take two shakes of a beagle's tail to pick up that literature on the rabies event. Maybe we should kill time by deciding what restaurant to pick. What kind of food do you like?"

"The kind of food that's prepared by somebody else. Remember that we have a canine sidekick with us. Maybe we could grab take-out and head for a well-lit park."

"Okay, let's see what we can make work. You brought a leash, right?"

She made a contented moan and nodded with her eyes closed.

Kemp headed down a straight-away and took a moment to steal a glimpse at her features. Makeup made her eyes more alluring, especially when she blinked. Since his typical encounter involved staring into the curly lashes of cocker spaniels, this date fell outside of regular. Well outside. Daring to risk admitting it, he opted for a compliment. "Delayne, you look nice tonight."

Eyes closed, her head rolled to one side. His passenger had fallen fast asleep.

~

The Mexican restaurant smelled of melted cheese and roasted peppers. Delayne enjoyed a distant view of the street fair though its noise was muffled by an indoor Spanish-speaking sound track. The manager had consented to the crated pup in his garden court, a deal Kemp managed to negotiate after being offered a free appetizer. No doubt the street fair's food trucks pilfered some business from the Main Street establishments tonight, so they became more accommodating to fight back. With two combination platters on the way, she hoped they'd made the right choice.

Kemp dribbled a few dry morsels of dog food into the puppy's crate. "Sorry about how fast that first bowl of tortilla chips disappeared. Guess I'm hungrier than I thought."

"I did my share of damage, too. I think they'll bring a new bowl when the queso dip comes. It's nice out here. With the tiny lights and potted plants, it has real ambience." She crossed her ankles and her foot struck his under the table.

He transformed from dog tender to date in a matter of seconds as he leaned across the table. "I don't hold it against you for falling asleep on the way up. You look more refreshed now, anyway."

"Sorry about that. I'm in a much better frame of

mind, I admit. Thanks for being such a good listener. My life has become a real soap opera lately."

"You're quite welcome." He sat straight when the server brought the appetizer in a wide-rimmed bowl with a cactus painted on it. A bowl of tortilla chips soon followed.

"From the looks of that steam coming off the queso, we'd better chat for a few more seconds. So, tell me, did I miss anything while dozing off?" She placed her napkin in her lap and hooked her brow at him.

"Well, the drop down into town happened all at once, so it was fairly dramatic. I didn't know which way to turn at first. Thanks again go to Tommy Lee, as he swiped the GPS unit out of the glove box, but I managed." A funny look swept his face, as though he'd remembered something more.

"What else aren't you telling me? I didn't make any clandestine confessions in my sleep, did I?" She dipped a chip and set it on the edge of her plate to cool.

"No, no bank robberies revealed, or anything like that." He glanced out at the revelry and then back at her. "You missed me saying how nice you look tonight. So there it is—a rehashed compliment from a geeky doctor whose training didn't include how to date a beautiful woman."

A classical guitar piece started over the speakers, causing his admission to land on her with comingled wonderment, the music with the words. She truly needed to bite that dipped chip to hide behind the artifice of eating, so the date portion of the evening wouldn't be in the forefront. She would be more comfortable laughing the moment away, but it seemed too genuine to make light of it. When her cheeks heated, she opted for a sip of water.

"I like this music. It seems to suit you—a roaming melody without words." He reached for a chip and began his assault on the appetizer.

"Now you're making reference to my circuitous survey route this morning…I don't know what Connors was thinking." She claimed her chip and soon had the smooth cheese dip between her lips. It was a spicy kind of delicious.

"From here on out, I'm going to ban certain such elements from our conversation, as you've awakened to another locale here in Hot Springs. We should fully enjoy it." He poked the point of a triangular chip at her before scraping it through the cheese pond.

"You're absolutely right. Banning accepted. And thank you for the compliment, though I think you might need your eyes checked. You see—or maybe you don't—but my hair length side-to-side is like the Bay of Fundy at low and high tides." She demonstrated the different lengths with her hands and discovered a portion of singed-off hair had escaped her braid job. Damage repair took a few seconds, all of which he watched in a direct stare.

"I've never been to the Bay of Fundy. The tidal surge must be…phenomenal."

"Me either, but I bet they have some late-spring seabird nesting on those cliffs, black sooty colonies on the rock ledges and whatnot."

"You like to bird watch casually, as well as conduct research then?"

"I enjoy every aspect. Someday I want a real home with a birdfeeder outside my kitchen window. You know, something long-term they can count on." She took another chip and scooped up a red pepper in the cheese sauce.

Kemp nodded and gave a brief smile before cramming a whole chip into his mouth.

"Lost Creek will do for now." She nibbled her chip as the server appeared with two steaming hot plates. After shifting her water glass to a safer location, she watched her meal alight right in front of her, a succulent feast. The musical piece's crescendo arrived as Kemp's plate landed on the table with aplomb. Their eyes met and time stood still until the final chord played.

"Let me bless the food," Kemp said, his head already bowed. His hand slid across the table palm up, an unspoken invitation to join him before the Lord.

Delayne received it as a threshold of sorts, to touch one another and go to God with it. After a momentary stomach flutter, she placed her hand in his and closed her eyes.

He curled his fingers around hers. "Lord, we thank you for time away from the ordinary routines we live and the chance to get to know each other a little better. We ask you to bless this food and the hands that prepared it. How fitting we should eat like royalty tonight, since we are children of the King. In the precious name of Jesus, amen."

She echoed the benediction, but knew she was far from being finished. When he squeezed her hand for release, she sensed a great reluctance to let go—so she didn't. A blush worked up from her neck and heated her cheeks. Overhead, the music filtered down interspersed with claps and cheers like a matador was performing great feats of bravery. Well, she might just join him.

A gray-haired lady in a blue pantsuit sauntered up to the table, her napkin twisted in her knotted hand. "I tell you, it's encouraging to see young people say grace in public. Even though I watch for it, I don't get to see it as much as I used to." She clucked her tongue in personal disappointment and began to walk out of the garden.

"Thank you, ma'am. Have a peaceful evening," Kemp replied.

Delayne pressed her thumb against his and waited for restoration of their privacy. Her throat constricted, but she plied through the condition to be true to what her heart desired in the moment. "Do you think you might be able to eat your dinner one-handed tonight?" She lifted her hand ever so slightly and spread her fingers apart.

With a discernible nod, he slid his fingers in the valley of hers and clamped them together. "If it makes this night last longer, then I'm all for eating slower." His amber gaze seemed lit with something new and intense.

The server stepped into view and lit the candle in the center of the table. "Your bill has just been paid in full, so stay and enjoy your meal as long as you like." He bowed and disappeared back inside.

Kemp blinked, shook his head, and looked up at her misty-eyed. "All that generosity just for praying. Does that seem right?"

She rubbed her thumb against his. "Sometimes, the communion with God yields perks beyond what we ask for."

"Like what we hope for?" His brow arched for a second and then he seemed to find his own answer. He tugged for possession of her hand, leaned in, and brushed a kiss across her knuckles.

The matador music had given way to a satiny song featuring a female vocalist who sang in a suggestive whisper. Undone by her trance, the translation seemed to transcend the heights of human experience. Delayne didn't know what was being said, but she sure recognized the feeling of allurement, and it fell with compelling capture from where she sat. *Mercy me. What a prayer.*

"This food's too hot. Dance with me, Layne," Kemp whispered. Without waiting for an answer, he drew her up by the hand and placed an arm around her shoulders.

A thousand "yes" responses held at bay, she tucked into his arms and let the singer set the mood. When he turned her deeper into an alcove of tall ferns, they could have been anywhere in the world. Her scope shrank to amber brown eyes and the velvety olive skin of his neck. The music slowed to the last few notes and her free hand ventured up from his shoulder to his chin. Unable to resist the pencil-thin chinstrap beard, she passed an admiring stroke his way.

Kemp's face hovered over hers for the briefest of seconds and then his lips sought hers for the final note. They landed as a glancing brush with almost no contact at all, a polite gesture.

"I don't believe you had that pressure right, Doc," she whispered. Her finger directed his chin back into the strike zone and she readily helped him with the adjusted application.

This time when they parted, his lips slid up to press against her forehead. "I think I found a sweet little birdie," he confessed, his tone affectionate.

The way her heart fluttered and took wing, Delayne was sure of it.

~

Midnight approached, but Kemp eased up on the gas pedal to make the ride home last. Delayne sat sideways in her seat curled around the puppy's cage. Yes, he had capitulated on the move up front, as long as Strappy stayed in its carrier. The pup couldn't cause an accident from there. Two carry-out boxes lent the car an onion-heavy aroma. The smell couldn't entice him further, as he was stuffed and content. He stole a glance at Delayne, who'd been quiet compared to the drive up.

A fast-approaching car came up from behind, its bright lights glaring in the mirror. He deflected the shine with the night vision adjustment and slowed, hoping to aid their pending pass. With the roads so curvy through this section, that might not happen for awhile.

Delayne stirred with the deceleration and looked out her window. "What is it, the sheriff? I have my seatbelt on, and you're well under the speed limit, so what gives?"

"It's not the sheriff. More likely a speed-driven liquor run. Harrison is in a dry county, so lots of locals come up to Hot Springs for their libations. At least that's the scuttlebutt I've heard. I slowed down to let them get by us, but the road's not cooperating."

She hummed in response. In a half-mile, they passed an informational sign. "There's a scenic lookout up ahead. Why don't we pull in to let them by?"

"Okay. We may see the lights of Harrison in the distance, but other than that, I don't know how scenic it will be." He hit the right turn signal and followed the exit lane off the main road. Within seconds, the hotrod laid rubber and rumbled its twin mufflers at him as it sped by.

"Kill the engine, will you? I want to see what's so scenic about this spot." She scooted up in her seat for a better vantage point.

"Sure thing. How's Scat-man-do behaving in there?"

"The puppy's been asleep most of the way, which is good. I don't need a pet that wakes me up at night, not with my schedule."

"Good point. If you see anything spectacular, please let me know." Though he squinted to make out a few pinpoints of light in the distance, an approaching car soon made that impossible. As he timed their arrival out of the corner of his eye, he sensed it was taking longer than necessary. The car had slowed down.

Delayne reached for her window crank. "At least it's peaceful up here. Let's give Mother Nature a listen, shall we?"

The car veered out of its lane toward them, its tires rolling slower.

Kemp thought otherwise. "Keep the window up. We've got company. I don't trust it." He sheltered his eyes from the headlights as the two front grills aligned.

Delayne turned toward him, her cheek flat against the seat back. "I don't trust it either, so I'm locking my door." She fisted the door lock and came right back to his side. In the dark, her fingers inched under his arm.

He clamped down tight to secure them as the other car jerked forward and began to maneuver past them at a creep. Through the windshield, he could make out the driver. It was Tommy Lee.

As the car passed, the driver's middle finger straightened from the wheel for an irreverent salutation. Several guys in the car burst out laughing.

Kemp had to think fast to send them a message of his own. He cocked his shoulders toward Delayne. "Throw your arms around my neck and lock that door behind me in one motion."

"Right," she replied, already lunging in compliance.

As soon as he heard the lock engage, he longed for the rest of the delivery. He brushed her unraveled braid back and caught her jawline with his thumbs. Despite a little gasp, Delayne fell willing victim to his impromptu plan. In the dark of the scenic overlook, the stolen kiss had a sweetness all its own. He upped the pressure a bit at the end, just to keep her happy.

The creeping car threw rocks under its tires and veered back onto the blacktop with the blare of a horn. In seconds, the threat vanished.

Delayne tucked the dog crate back in her lap. "Who would be headed to Hot Springs at this late hour?"

"Young bucks looking for trouble, I suppose." He wiped his upper lip and kept an eye on the rearview mirror as the shrinking taillights disappeared beyond the far curve. Under the distinct impression they thought his car had been abandoned along the road, the implications haunted him.

"Hey, I like the way you shielded me in the thick of things. Nice move."

He started the engine and flicked on the lights. "Good, then I won't have to apologize."

"Well, shame on me for liking it. Does that make me too easy?"

"No, little bird." He rested a hand on her trembling knee and steered back onto the highway. The buzz fed by his growing attraction tried to ease the taut vise clamping his chest, but the sight of Tommy Lee on the prowl a good distance from Ponca wouldn't allow it. The weight of the late hour began to press on him like a rockslide.

"Can we go paddling on the river tomorrow, after I sleep late?"

"I can't think of anything else I'd rather do." He gave her knee a squeeze. "How about I pick you up at one o'clock?"

"Perfect. I'll eat breakfast for lunch before you get there." She wrapped his arm in a hug and nestled against his shoulder, as much as the pet carrier would allow.

With Delayne in such proximity, Tommy Lee's effect on him diminished like the pinpoint of vanishing taillights. Kemp had the sensation of falling off a ledge, but the landing had a marshmallow feel to it. When her hair brushed his cheek, he gave her a quick kiss along the part that ran through it. *Bay of Fundy, indeed.* He was over the cliff—one he never knew existed—and falling headlong toward a big splash.

Chapter 7

To Kemp, the river from Pruitt on downstream unfolded in a total explore. Tilted tablets of rock spilled from the shrubby banks. In reptile-lovers heaven, he'd never seen so many snakes basking in one place. He laughed when Delayne had given him instructions to steer down the centerline of the waterway. To make her a better-rounded animal lover, he might have to work on that snake avoidance tendency.

She pointed her dripping paddle tip at the rock wall comprising the west bank. "Look, cliff swallows. They're dancing in the wind."

"Good analogy. It reminds me of our dance last night." He held his steering stroke in the water too long, and the canoe cocked toward the opposite bank. Distracted by the memory, he wondered how to repeat the magic of such an unguarded embrace. The canoe glided way beyond the centerline and headed for a rock slab.

Delayne skipped a stroke and glanced back over her shoulder. "Captain, you're strong to starboard. Are you daydreaming back there?" When the puppy shook her yellow flip-flop, she made an unsuccessful grab to salvage it.

"Maybe. A man in my position has a lot to consider. You know, like which can of beans to open for supper tonight, survival-type matters of that nature." He hooked a J-stroke and corrected the canoe to midstream.

"Beans? Oh, drat. I had hoped to invite you over for homemade pork egg rolls cooked on my wok. That hardly compares to your dear old stash of beans. I could probably ask one of those concessionaires to take your place—if you're booked and all."

Not willing to let her invitation slip by, Kemp jabbed the water's surface and kicked up a fair-sized splash. It landed right between her shoulder blades. "Can we reconsider that invitation again? I mean both parts—the start, where you really mean it, and the ending, where I say, 'yes, I'd love to.'"

Delayne stopped paddling and swung around backwards on the seat to directly address him. With a tug of her visor, she straightened her spine. "Hey Kemp. More than anything, I'd like you to stay for dinner at Lost Creek tonight and help me stuff some egg rolls to fry on my wok. We'll make a mountain of them, so you can take some leftovers home with you. If any of this sounds good to you, please say you'll come to dinner." She cupped her hand into the river and spilled some liquid turquoise onto the base of her throat.

"It *all* sounds good to me so, yes, I'd like to come

for dinner. Thank you." Buoyed by a continuance of their day together, he took a power stroke and the whole boat rocked.

"That settles it then. We both have something to look forward to. Now, let's book it out of Snakeville so I can swim. It already feels like June out here. I'm roasting." She scooped her hand in the river again, but instead of wearing it, she slung it at him.

Not in a mood to let bygones be bygones, he retaliated with several heavy splashes. *That should help her bide her time until the dunk.*

Delayne resumed her paddling position with a laugh and settled into rhythmic strokes. The water hue deepened in the shadow of a towering bluff ahead and her attention seemed drawn to it.

Kemp allowed the canoe a subtle wander in that direction, a maneuver that soon placed them in the shade.

"I think there are more shadows on the river this afternoon, at least through here. What a break from the sun." She pulled her visor off and doused it in the water. "I really need to go in."

"Hold on. Let's see what's around the bend up ahead. The map shows a switchback to the northwest."

"Okay. I'll give you five minutes to find the best spot ever."

"I accept that challenge. Hey, does it strike you as crazy? The northward flow of the river, I mean." When the pup tried to launch a flip-flop, he pinned the shoe with his paddle tip and made a warning click in his teeth. Like a good trainee, the juvenile delinquent relented.

"To be truthful, I had to study it on the topo map

before I fully comprehended it. The Buffalo River is one of only a handful on the entire continent to head off north."

"It's a river that goes its own way. You've got to respect that."

"I do respect the river, but it's these limestone bluffs that really wow me." She glanced up the crevassed rock as though to pay immediate tribute to her inspiration.

"I get that. I sure do. And as you so astutely alluded to once before—taller is better." Kemp stifled his grin at the personal reference, but when she turned around, he gave her the full five-dollar smile.

"Men," she muttered with a shake of her head. Her paddle soon slapped the water to resume business.

Now under a time clock for their next stop, Kemp began to scan both sides of the river for retreat potential. Nothing departed from the norm on the far side—a shrub-lined bank with an occasional jutted rock. Maybe he should allow her a close-up inspection of her beloved bluff.

They rounded the bend to open waters ahead. A scream pierced the air followed by a cannonball's plunging splash. When a figure stood atop a fifteen-foot high rock diving platform, he rose in a crouch. The daredevil flung himself off the rock with a rebel yell and made the plunge feet first. "We are so doing that." He shrugged off his T-shirt and flung it at Delayne.

"Wait…I only wanted to swim."

With no time left to negotiate, he crept up the hull until he reached the center brace. He patted the dog and gave it his "stay" hand command. "Meet me up there, Layne. I want you with me when I jump." And with that, he hefted his overheated frame over the gunwale into the milky green water of the Buffalo.

~

Clad in only her swimsuit, Delayne made the climb trying to avoid the unforgiving limbs of hardwood trees lining the bank. The well-trodden path held a few exposed roots as hazards, and her bare feet celebrated once on the towering rock. Certain there was no way to talk him of this, she gathered her courage and searched out the best route up the rock face.

Once she'd cleared the top plateau, she spotted Kemp a step back from the diving edge. She tucked a loose hair back under her visor and immediately wished she'd left it in the boat with her sunglasses. With the puppy in destruct mode, nothing in the boat was safe. When they were ready to dive, she'd loop it around her arm for safekeeping.

Kemp's shoulders rolled forward as his hands clasped under his chin in prayer position. He stepped back from the edge and bowed his head.

Not ready for such a show of masculine humility, Delayne let the scene work to soften her attitude. At angel altitude above the scenic river, she hadn't given God a thought. The Creator was due some consideration for a masterpiece such as this. She headed for the rear of the rock and took a few seconds for a praise-filled prayer. The breeze lofted around her and— for a split second—she felt as if she could fly.

A quick glance at Kemp spoke the exact opposite. His face appeared leaden, almost statue-like. He finally cracked his plastered expression by blowing out a breath. His cheeks puffed out like a toad in the process. Was he dealing with something?

She tiptoed across the wet surface and stood beside him. A quick assessment yielded more questions than answers. When his gaze finally locked on hers, it bore part of the explanation—the apprehension portion. "Hey, what gives?"

"I'm not sure." He blew out another breath. Toad cheeks came and went. "Somewhere on the way up, my gumption turned to jelly, I guess. The water seems…further away when you're up here looking down."

Delayne stepped to the edge and leaned out to examine his description first-hand. The water only seemed to beckon with its blue-green allure. "No, it can't be more than fourteen feet down, if that. This is a solid cliff, not crumbly like the ones along the logging road I had to cross. The river has been polishing this rock for thousands of years. And the pool is deep below. See how much darker the water is along this bank?"

At the mere suggestion, he clamped his eyelids closed. His tanned forearms soon folded across his midsection. "Better not oversell it."

"Oh, right." She stepped back beside him and let her shoulders nudge his. Without a shadow of doubt, his immobility reflected a fear of heights. She would have to play coach from here on out, or they'd never make it to the water. The back of her neck radiated with the sun's full force. Since Kemp stood like a blind man, she'd start his handicapped accommodation there.

She took his arm in both hands with as much gentleness as she could muster. Next, for the Braille translation, she pressed her lips onto his bulging bicep. "Remember back in the boat when you said you wanted me with you when you jumped?"

A slight nod led into a full-fledged neck roll, as he seemed to try working the kinks out. Despite the movement, his eyes failed to open.

"Well, I traipsed up here behind you because it landed on me like an honor—to be the one asked to stand up here with you, Doctor Kemp Junkowski, DVM. And here we are, right in God's full sight, side-by-side. He sculpted this cliff over the eons, just like he knit you together into a tall specimen of a man. In fact, you're almost half the length of this rock to the water. If you stretch out, you'll be halfway down from the get-go."

"I don't know about that."

She relocated her lips to his padded shoulder, as high as she could reach. The sun had heated the spot unmercifully, so she laid her cool cheek against his roasting skin. The word "trust" echoed through her thoughts so she wrapped her argument around it. "So, what if this cliff-top challenge represents a trust issue for us? Part One, you asked me to come with you—and I did. Part Two, I'm asking you to jump with me. If you could step past this…hesitation for me, would you be willing to—in your heart-of-hearts—do it?"

He sucked in an audible breath, but left the toad cheeks out this time. His eyes fluttered open and he glanced out at the edge.

"God as our witness, in weakness and in strength. Let's do this together, Kemp, and make an unforgettable memory." With confident insistence, Delayne slid her palm down into his. When he clutched it, she gave a squeeze back.

"I must be crazy," he replied. His lips tucked into

one cheek. "How about on three?"

"This is your thing, so you count. Are we running from here?"

"Yes, running. One, two… three." He broke into motion, his hand locked on hers like a vice-grip.

She pushed off with fervor and in three steps went airborne. For a glorious moment, she became a magnificent bird that soared over a river spanning the land like an agate necklace. Her partner glanced her way right before impact. He wore a breathtaking smile, having made his peace with gravity somewhere along the way.

~

More relaxed than imaginable, Kemp rolled the cabbage mix inside the wrapper, using care to keep the filling contained. The counter looked like a culinary war zone, much to his credit. He would soon enjoy the spoils of victory in his battle over hunger, as the first eggroll spattered in the wok. It smelled sumptuous.

Delayne slid the fingerbowl full of cornstarch water closer to him. "That lump may be a problem. See if you can smooth it down before you seal the wrapper."

"That lump is really a hunk of pork that I personally will annihilate, so call this one mine." He plunged his index finger into the water bowl and ran it across the edge of the tempura wrapper. The pressed seal came off flawless.

"Hmmm. Someone's being artistic—in a starving sort of way." She turned to the wok and used a fan-shaped spatula to roll the current victim over. The oil spattered around the crisping treat. She began to hum a happy tune.

Kemp delivered his masterpiece to the platter and

lined up his next subject. "Hey, aren't these eggrolls considered appetizers?"

Delayne gave a curt laugh and left the range to search for something in the fridge door. She stood with a rose-colored bottle of sauce. "Not tonight they aren't. An appetizer is merely a taste of something, but this is our main course."

"Why? Because we're going to eat a lot?" He leveled two heaping spoonfuls of filling dead center on the wrapper. The puppy at his ankle whined, so he shook the floppy leather shoestrings on his deck shoes. The canine lunged for them right away.

Delayne poured the sauce into a shallow bowl. "Right. We're not tasting…we're eating a ton. Try to keep up."

He rolled the small square and sealed it to perfection. "Watch out, lady. The surgeon is now operating in the kitchen. Look at this—I'm a natural, right?"

She laughed and placed a double layer of paper towels over a large plate. "Yes, sir, Doc. You're on full throttle now. Our test bundle is coming out of the wok, so get ready to hand me your first creation." She scooped the crispy-shelled eggroll out of the oil, drained it for a few seconds, and landed it on the blotter.

"I can't believe how hungry being out on the river makes me." He roared like a lion and pulled another wrapper from the stack.

"Hand me the next one. We've got to keep them coming, in and out of the wok, to maintain the oil temperature."

He eased the platter over to the rim of the range to

make his stash easier to reach. "This way you can grab one when you're ready. I'll roll and load them like a cook-bot."

"Improved efficiency. I like it." The oil popped when the eggroll made landfall inside the wok's curved basin. She retracted her hand to move from harm's way inside the splatter zone. "Tell me, did you have a good time this afternoon on our float?" Her voice sounded melodic.

He gave the tie on the front of her apron a tug. "Yes, an extremely good time, thanks to you. Guess you could have left me up there on that diving rock, all alone and knock-kneed."

She batted her lashes in response. Two dimples soon appeared on her cheeks. "Since you placed your invaluable trust in little ole me, I couldn't go orphaning you just because of a minor…hesitation on high."

He focused on the roll-up maneuver and created another edible masterpiece. Dexterity he could readily share. Deeper revelations proved more difficult. He struggled with how much to admit, as openness led to vulnerability. Still wanting to impress her, he had no intention of coloring himself weak.

Delayne leaned closer to cut the cooked eggroll with a knife. She glanced his way with unguarded interest. Steam rose from the hot filling and carried the aroma across the counter.

A harmless angle occurred to him, so he approached the flawed subject. "My mother claims I was always careful with my posture as a kid. Hence, when I learned activities like riding a bike, it came as more of a challenge. I reveled in the balanced part, but the crashes, not so much. I became a stickler for precision to protect against the inevitable wipeout.”

She nodded with the disclosure. “I bet you were a darling—just not on roller skates.” She dipped a portion of the eggroll in the rosy sauce and lifted it to his mouth.

More than ready to stop talking and eat, he bent and nibbled it out of her hand. A melding of unbelievable flavors exploded onto his taste buds, a crunchy-sweet endeavor. “Mmmm, so good,” he managed.

“The plum sauce is a nice complement, I think, but the pork-cabbage-carrot combination steals the show.” She nipped the end of the remaining portion after dipping it through the sauce.

“Don’t forget the onion. Man, I need to keep making these. Try not to distract me, cook.”

She giggled and stepped over to tend the wok. A sizzle soon followed.

Kemp widened his stance to work lower on the counter. The butterball puppy rolled across the tile floor with his foot shift. It gave a halfhearted yelp, righted itself, and came straight back to chew his laces. Something about the cozy hands-on activity and the blend of down-home camaraderie began to tug on his heartstrings. He craved more genuine quality in his life. Maybe this was a great place to start. When Delayne appeared at his side to offer another bite of the test appetizer, it generated a want for a different fix.

“I bet you can’t…”

He locked his arm around her shoulder in a magnetic trap. “I bet I can,” he readily replied. He dodged the food offering and went right for her lips. She tasted of plum sauce and kissed with above-average spirit for a shanghaied cook. A loud pop from the wok soon broke them apart.

Delayne wiped her lips with the back of her hand as she scooted toward the range. In seconds, she had retrieved the eggroll and deposited it on the blotter. She beckoned for another. "You need to get cranking in the production department, Kemp."

"Balance. Strive for balance." He flashed a wink at the wok tender, wet his fingertip, and sealed his next cabbage-filled candidate. When she returned with another crispy morsel, he partook of it with a monster-sized gobble.

She shook her head, her eyes full of mirth. "At least one of us could roller skate."

He worked the food into one cheek to reply. "Good training…if you wanted to grow up to be a car hop." He chewed and let her think about it.

Busy with the cleanup, she rummaged around the counter. When she found a long-handled wooden spoon, she seemed pleased. After baby-talking the pup, she strolled behind him and slapped a love tap onto his back pocket.

Distracted from his task, he caught her elbow as she passed. "How much time before the next one's done, Layne?"

Her hazel eyes sparked as an eyebrow shot up. "Enough."

With that, he took advantage of the cook again, delighted that she came to him on tiptoe—a tempting appetizer from a different menu. This time, he played deaf to the spatter in the wok and the chronic gnawing underfoot. The embrace lent balance—and then some.

~

Delayne closed the book on their post-dinner

reading session and watched Kemp play with the puppy nestled on his chest. Those two were growing an enviable attachment, and they weren't the only ones. How could she tell Kemp she'd like to see more of him without sounding like a moonstruck teenager? She was twenty-seven and directionless, as she'd never been down this road of affinity before.

"James Herriot is inspirational. Thanks for reading some to me. It makes me want to recommit myself to my veterinarian work. Not that I ever doubted, but this location has proven a real struggle for me. Did I tell you I have a new mentor? He's giving me some common sense pointers about building up a practice, slow and steady."

"Sounds like good advice. How did you two meet?" She leaned her shoulder against the sofa and rested her back. From the feel of it, she'd likely be sore from all the paddling tomorrow.

"It's kind of a mail-order bride relationship right now. He sent me a congratulatory note for opening the Harrison clinic and offered to mentor me. I wrote right back with twenty-odd questions about what to invest in, how to drum up business, and such. I'm hoping to hear back from him this coming week." The puppy made a guttural growl, and Kemp clamped both hands on it for more roughhousing.

"What's his name? Maybe I've heard of him."

"Doctor Gaylord. He's out of Eustace Springs, north of here." He boxed Strappy's ears when it snapped at his chin.

A trickle of embarrassment shot down Delayne's neck. She covered the name on the book's spine and slid it under the sofa's skirt. She'd cross that bridge when she could count on the planks beneath them being strong enough to bear the weight. Right now, she simply wanted unfettered time together, a string of dates. "He sounds nice. Maybe he can send you some business by referral."

"Hey, I never thought of that. I guess it could happen." He rolled onto one side and faced her. "Listen, I need to see this puppy more frequently. It's a real handful. If you're coming into town most days, I'd like to have it at the clinic with me. That's more productive than being left out here alone, anyway. Strappy's in total destruct mode when left to his own devises."

Delayne looked away to consider the request. She couldn't let him see it, but it hurt that his focus was on the dog, not her. The night drew to a close and they didn't even have their next date scheduled, for pity's sake. She closed her eyes and let out a little groan of contemplation. A hand soon clamped around the cap of her left shoulder and drifted into a thumb-pressed massage. "Oh, way too sore back there." She sucked in a breath and let the muscle kneading do its painfully good work.

"Tactical flaw," he replied in a soft tone. "I forgot about balance." The puppy yipped as he sat it on the floor.

Delayne trapped her knees against her chest before Strappy could occupy her lap. Kemp's other hand soon started on the opposite shoulder blade, her preferred rowing side. The muscles were undeniably tied in knots. She sat wordless as the twin circular sensations sent ripples down her spine. With just the right amount of pressure, the doctor sure knew how to administer the treatment. His prolonged touch seemed to heal the heart-hurt birthed only moments before.

Kemp's hands clamped the tops of her shoulders and pulled her back against the couch's padded cushion. "There is some impressive musculature back here, miss. I bet you could bench press a Labrador with these babies." He worked on the tops of her shoulders next.

She rocked to and fro under the rhythmic pressure. Between the teasing and the touch, she lost her emotional equilibrium. Instead of chuckling at his dog-lifting inference, tears welled in her eyes, so she squeezed them shut. This evening would not end with her falling to pieces over regret for her innate inability to attract the opposite gender, not if she could help it. A prayer lifted from her spirit straight toward heaven, a plea for guidance and some mutual meeting of the minds and hearts. At the end, she gave a tiny sob.

Kemp's forearms stretched across the base of her throat which led to a giant hug from behind. He nestled his face into the crook of her neck and stayed there long enough to draw several breaths against her skin. "So sweet," he whispered. He rubbed his jawline against the side of her cheek and held her.

"We need to do something about this," she whispered. "I don't even know when I'm going to see you again." She tightened her core muscles, but couldn't keep one tear from betraying her toughness as it slid down her cheek.

He kissed it away and dropped his chin onto her shoulder. "You're the best thing about my move to Harrison. God sure has a way of getting a man's attention when he's on his knees. If the business was doing only half as good as this...personal endeavor…I'd be one highly successful veterinarian." He gave her another lengthy squeeze.

She decided to get the grievance out in front for discussion. "So you want to spend more time with my puppy?"

He answered with a groan. "That's not a fair lead-off. You deserve a well-behaved pet, one that minds your commands. I have the time right now and the know-how to train him. And Chinstrap's decent company during clinic hours to help make the day pass when business is light. That's more days than not at this point, so we have time for each other."

She couldn't argue his rationale. In fact, she should offer to pay him for the training. But she knew this wasn't about money. It was about priorities. Evidently, she wasn't one. Self pity drove a shudder down her length. She released her knees to get up. Maybe movement would break this defeatist spell. When she tried to get up, Kemp would have none of it.

"Before you fly away, let's talk about you and me, little bird."

"Is there a 'you and me?' We've had one dinner date and two floats down the river." She choked down a sob.

"All memorable. Do you dare trust me with more? You know my situation here. If the clinic fails, I don't have a fall-back plan." He rested his forehead on her shoulder.

"I'm not trying to date your clinic, Kemp. Can't you separate the two?" She exhaled in disgust. This argument wasn't leaving the ground and she knew it.

His head jerked up. "You want to date me? Like regular dating, I mean? Is that what you're saying?"

There was the truth, right behind her, languid on the couch. He had no sense of direction due to lack of intention, an emotional desert. *Could the whole thing be a royal waste of time and effort?* Her head started to spin at the possibility. How could she possibly respond? Seconds ticked by and no honest answer availed itself.

Kemp shifted his grip to her waist and hoisted her onto the couch's edge with one fell swoop of masculine power. His hands sought hers and his fingers soon slid between hers. "Let me get this said. Layne, nothing makes me happier than being with you. Please don't draw back now. I'd be head-over-heels to date you. Honest, I would. From my heart to yours, what do you say?" He spread his fingers as though lending her freedom to choose.

She fiddled with the collar of his T-shirt. "It's not about the clinic?"

"Not at all."

She ran a knuckle up the side of his neck. "Not about the dog training?"

His honeyed gaze focused all the more. "Not about any dog."

Her fingertip caught the slender line of his beard and slid down to his chin. "I think I'd like that opportunity—to date and see where this goes. You…you're enigmatic to me, Kemp. Not only do you stand above the others…but you stand apart with your integrity."

"Well, how's this for the truth?" He slid one arm around her back and pulled her closer. "Every time you walk into a room, I can't take my eyes off of you. Even that day under the tent, the tear in your jeans struck me as fascinating. Whenever you touch me, that effect magnifies."

She placed her palms on his chest to approximate the placement of the AED paddles. "Would you like me to jumpstart your cardiac arrest, Doctor Junkowski?"

"Only if the patient needs salvaging, in your estimation." He blinked in willing surrender. "Should I keep my eyes shut to help you focus?"

The distance between them closed. "I believe it's too late for that. Now, hold on while I save your life." She administered aid to safeguard her dating prospects, a most worthwhile effort.

Chapter 8

With Strappy thrashing against the leash, Kemp approached the front door of the popcorn shop, a review of his strategy revolving in his thoughts. *No popcorn, only information.* He had two weeks to get his offer on paper stock to hand out at the Memorial Day vaccination event. He would have preferred to be out on the river with Delayne that holiday, but commitments counted. That impression of being a public servant would be a boost for business, no doubt.

After shortening the leash, he pulled the door open. The aroma of candied popcorn hung in the air. Used to the disinfectant smell at the clinic, he'd become a fat man if this was his normal atmosphere. Still, the candy saturation lent the place a vacationland aura.

A middle-aged woman with bushy red hair reported to the front counter. Her expression softened when she spotted the puppy. "Good morning. How can I help you two? I've just made some caramel popcorn, if I could make a suggestion."

"Well, I was hoping you could make more of a recommendation. I'm Kemp Junkowski, the new veterinarian two blocks over on Second Street. I received your postcard flyer in last week's mail and recognized the benefit of such a broad-brush outreach. Could you tell me who your printer is?" Strappy sniffed at some confections on a side shelf so he bent and tucked the little thief into his arms.

"Sure, I used Miller's Print and Engraving on Spring Street. He gave me a bulk deal on five hundred. I think it totaled around thirty-seven dollars in all for the printing. He runs two images per full sheet and then cuts them in half. I chose to address the cards myself, but they offer a service for that, as well."

"Thanks, that seems reasonable. I have a special event coming up Memorial Monday. It's called 'Cures for Canines' and promotes low-cost rabies vaccinations. I plan to use the postcard as a promotional tool that includes a discount for the first office visit for new clients."

She leaned her chin on her elbows. "I heard some of the downtown merchants were planning sidewalk sales that day. Maybe you should set up out front and try to catch some passing foot traffic. People are dog crazy around here. You can bet they'll have them out and about on the holiday. Did you think about listing your event in the newspaper?"

"No, I hadn't. Would they do that? It's a state-wide event." The idea appealed to him, but the potential cost sure didn't.

"Yes, they have a local happenings page in the Friday paper. They run it as a community service, so it's free. You probably have just enough time to make the deadline for listing it. I've got yesterday's paper around here somewhere, if you need it."

"I do, thank you very much. You're just a fount of useful information." A beeper sounded in back that caused the dog to squirm. He clamped his free hand on its head to corral any mischievous intent.

"Sorry, I need to step back and get that timer. I have a batch of cinnamon popcorn ready now. It's been popular lately. Must be a summer thing. Be right back with the paper." She disappeared off one side of the counter and pans soon started to rattle in the back.

Kemp looked around the narrow shop. The owner had diversified her selections to include hard candy and other miscellaneous treats that had a longer shelf life than popcorn. That made good sense for a snack store. He wished he could give her some business and take a sack with him, but spare money was nonexistent this week.

She returned with a white bag open at the top. With a flourish, she pulled the rolled-up newspaper from her back pocket and slapped it onto the counter. "I tucked a copy of my mailing list inside the paper for your use. It also occurred to me that you were entitled to the free sample on your first visit, since you received my postcard. So here's the cinnamon popcorn, hot out of the kettle. Cute puppy, by the way."

"Cute speckles maybe, but its cuddle has sharp teeth. It belongs to my girlfriend, so I get training duty." He laughed and gave Strappy's ears a rub. Reaching for the newspaper, he caught her gaze and thought there seemed some unfinished business on her mind. "I sure appreciate all the help today. Was there something else, like a pet problem, by any chance?"

"No, sakes alive. I don't have a pet. Well, things are settling down now, but that first year in business, life was all work and no play. It took me awhile to figure some things out."

"Right. Business is thin for the clinic right now, but I'm counting on it picking up by late summer. Wish I could diversify in the interim, you know, like hard candy on the shelf."

She laughed. "That's for the non-popcorn lovers. I'd push some products your way, but I don't think handling pets and throwing popcorn in your mouth tie together too well for your clientele." She stood a little straighter and soon snapped her fingers. "Wait a minute. My niece in Western Grove told me she's interested in bringing her mobile dog washing business to Harrison one day a week. She needs a steady location so people know where to find her. All it would cost you is water. Would you be interested?"

Kemp let the possibility of sharing his clinic space wash over his analytical mind. It would have to be worthwhile monetarily, or be more of a favor. "How successful has she been?"

"Golly, she's swamped—and she loves the work. She's a real go-getter and likes the tactile jobs, so messy dog hair isn't a problem. Let me give you her business card." She rummaged through a nearby drawer to find it.

A loss of control nagged his thoughts. Still, he couldn't let this opportunity escape his grasp, if it held the promise of gain. What's more, there could be some crossover business, as her customers could become his clients. They might even make it convenient, like a discount office visit with a grooming session attached. The possibilities began to unfurl.

"Oh, here it is. 'Pails & Tails Doggie Wash.' Isn't that just darling? I helped Becca with the name, of course. She designed the pup-in-the-bucket logo to go with it. Give her a call. You never know where it could lead."

Kemp thought better of it. "Do you have a pen? I want to leave my clinic number with you. Tell your niece we met and, if she's interested, have her call me. In the meantime, I'll research subsidiary business ventures and see what the standard cost-share is. There would have to be a per day hook-up fee of some sort. I want this venture to work for both parties."

"Aha. You're learning the number one rule for going into business. Pay yourself first. I respect that, and I'll make sure Becca respects it, too. Best of luck to you, Doc." She crinkled the top of the popcorn bag closed and slid it across the counter. "Don't forget your treat."

"You mean lunch." He laughed and gave her a nod. "Thanks for everything. I'll head down to Miller's and get this card thing going. I took pictures of the puppy this morning. Strappy's my cover model."

"Good choice. I wish popcorn was cute like that. Guess you have to work with what you've been given."

"Well, I won't get any return business because someone thought the clinic tasted great, either." He wrinkled his nose as though to prove it.

"Touché. Hey, if I'm out on Memorial Day, I'll check by to see how your canine event is fairing."

"Please do. I admit that day might make for a fine kick-off for the doggie wash concept, if we can get that negotiated to suit both parties."

"I'll throw that into my persuasive discussion then. Becca's determined to hook up somewhere, so expect her call. I'm Liv, by the way."

"Please call me Kemp, or Doctor Junk. My last name is tricky for some people."

"Thanks, Kemp. I have enough on my mind already, but these new ideas keep popping up. Such a distraction." She shook her head, but her eyes smiled.

"They call that 'business savvy' where I come from. And your popcorn bucket is brimming with it. I should be so lucky."

"You'll be fine, young man. You have to put in your time to get things cranking, that's all. Do your best work up front, and it will grow from there." Another beeper sounded in back. "Oh, great. The mocha is done. Gotta go. Ha! I made this batch for me. Everybody has a vice."

Kemp chuckled and turned for the door. Strappy squirmed to get down so he shoved the door open and let it reacquaint with the sidewalk. In seconds, a puddle filled the crack and watered a curbside weed. Crisis averted. They headed for Spring Street and an advertising break-through. When the urge struck, he stole a nibble from the bag. The cinnamon rode the popcorn crunch for a delightful balance of flavor. He'd have to go back, but first, he needed some cash flow. Delayne would like this popcorn, for sure. He only hoped she had a few kernels left to try.

~

Delayne fidgeted in her seat. The Monday staff meeting landed like a leaden waste of time on her bird survey schedule. Manning wandered around the room as though he couldn't collect his thoughts this morning. *Something must be up.* When Ross Connors entered with a dour face, it cinched the supposition. She glanced around the room to see who else might be involved.

The contents of the room appeared to be all male except for her. Funny, they had started the internship season with three other females. Had she missed her chance to give them an encouraging word? A raucous laugh rippled from the back. She turned and spotted Tommy Lee as the source. Timber sat beside him. When she made eye contact, the big guy wiped a gaping grin off his face and gave a tentative wave.

Connors shouldered up to Manning and they exchanged a few words. Manning shook his head and diverted to the front. A plain-faced young woman with brutally straight bangs followed him and took the corner seat. Manning cleared his throat and the room grew quiet. "Good morning, ladies and gentlemen."

"What about the rest of us?" an anonymous voice called from the back.

"Okay, welcome earthlings," Manning said, with a squint of one eye. "It's the third week of May and we expect visitation in the park to increase right up through Memorial weekend. The water level makes for good paddling right now, which is more than we can say for the summer months. You know the general public can get careless in a heartbeat, so please uphold all safety rules—and enforce them as necessary. Specifically, check for life jackets and PFDs in every boat that puts in."

"What about alcohol on the river, sir?" Timber called from the back.

"You all know the rules. No bottles or glass containers. No underage drinking, period. Make them show ID if there's any question. Watch the large groupings of tube floaters. Imbibers can pass out and still float along, as we've evidenced in the past. Pull them off and sober them up before releasing them to rejoin their buddies. Bottom line—prevent drownings due to alcohol consumption. I think that's clear enough."

"Should we go over the new vehicle use protocol?" Ross Connors asked.

"Right. It seems that we've been victimized over the weekend in the department motor pool. Again. We'll have to tighten down access, starting today through the remainder of summer. Interns, if you want to check out a vehicle for work-related use or need to trailer a boat, a senior member of staff has to sign off on it first."

A general moan surfaced after Manning's announcement. Delayne took her head in her hands and propped her elbows on the desktop. She needed four-wheel drive for her survey routes, no question. Now she'd have to give up her compound key and get permission. With her early hours, that wouldn't be easy.

"Talk to me afterwards if you need an exception," Manning added.

Delayne raised two fingers in the air to signify interest. She gave him a no-nonsense look.

The department head nodded. "Let's get on with the next matter. While water levels are adequate, we're launching a resource management project with the university's help. Last year's flood event made it all too clear that we've got some unaddressed erosion issues adversely affecting water quality on the river. Since we've got indigenous fish spawning and a few endangered crustaceans depending on non-turbid conditions, the time has come to face the matter. I'd like to introduce Eva Norman, an incoming grad student at University of Arkansas, who'll be focusing her research on the Buffalo. Eva, please come say a brief word to our staff."

Stiff as a board, the young woman unfolded from her seat and joined him up front. "As a native of Arkansas, I grew up floating this river. In fact, when I saw the park service grant listed for this erosion study, I selected it over several other options. Photography has been a hobby since I was fifteen, so naturally I wanted to incorporate it in my research project. For this assignment, I'll photo-document the erosion sites on the Buffalo, recommend stabilization priorities, and follow-up with another round of photographs after the site work is completed."

"That's it in a nutshell, folks," Manning said. "We want the photography done at water level, not from the opposing bank. I've divided the river up into three sections. Eva will need a float partner for each, so I'm asking for an intern volunteer per section. Upper river will be first, so who's game?" Manning held his hands up as though God would fill them with adequate help. Not a sound could be heard.

Delayne drew a silent breath and watched the young researcher grow uncomfortable. With her own research heading for a lull, she probably had spare time. A fleeting thought of Kemp surfaced and faded. She should commit and work romance around the float schedule, at least for a short duration. "I'm available the rest of May, so I volunteer.”

“Thank you Delayne,” Manning replied. “That covers the upper river from Ponca to Pruitt.”

“Can I trade that service for permission to keep my motor pool compound key? You know nobody wants to get up at three in the morning to let me in, chief.” She gave him a little grin and shrugged her shoulders.

“Permission granted. I’ll sign off on your key myself.” Manning slapped his hands together and regarded the group. “That takes us to midriver. Raise your hand if you’re stationed at Pruitt. Raise ‘em and hold ‘em high.”

Delayne looked back to see that a dozen hands rose halfway. Only Timber had the guts to fully acknowledge his duty. That figured. The rest didn’t want to be bothered with some camera gal on special assignment, no matter how important her research might prove.

Manning shifted his stance, but not his gaze. “Okay, I’ll take a volunteer first. Does anyone volunteer for the midriver float for the erosion study?”

Every hand went down—except Timber’s.

“Okay, Tim Price gets the assignment.”

Having worked with Timber on land, Delayne could only imagine what his bulk might be like in a narrow boat afloat on the winding river. Still, he had initiative, and that counted for something. Plus, he’d been a good assistant to her for the AED demonstration.

“Lastly, lower river. Again, a show of hands for all interns assigned to lower river, please.” Manning waited with his hands pressed together for the contingent in back to cooperate. After a few seconds, some progress occurred. “Right, now who wants to volunteer?"

Delayne tensed when someone uttered a sexist remark as all the hands lowered to dodge the extra duty. She could only imagine what Eva must be feeling. Too bad she hadn't brought an undergraduate assistant with her from the university. Maybe the grant wasn't deep enough.

A motion caught the corner of her eye about the time Eva raised a hand to point out a candidate. There sat Tommy Lee, his hand propped up in the air by the puppet strings of Satan himself. A flirtatious grin soon surfaced on his face. When she glanced back up front, Eva appeared pleased.

"All right then," Manning said. "We have Tommy Lee Resnick for the lower river segment. If you three volunteers would report up here after the meeting, we'll work through a tentative schedule. There will be some overnight campouts where access is limited. No worries, the department has camping gear for that. Thank you, Ms. Norman. You may be seated. Now let's talk about our next training course coming up Thursday—water rescues."

Another general moan filled the room. Delayne thought to switch her survey schedule to Tuesday and Thursday and ditch this next session. She'd talk it over with Manning, but she wasn't a seasonal intern like the rest. Her avian research had priority.

Eva glanced at her across the front row and gave her a friendly nod. Her skin seemed almost translucent, with the bridge of her nose dotted with freckles. Two perfect black arches crested over a pair of trusting blue eyes, all of which seemed highlighted by ridiculously short bangs that lent her the appearance of a tween.

A little worry niggled from deep inside Delayne's chest. The full length river float seemed less like a research endeavor, the more she processed it. She sighed, but the sliver of worry didn't fade. The phrase "overnight campouts" left her ill at ease. Timber could be trusted, but God and his heavenly choir knew that Tommy Lee could not. No, the angels would not rejoice over that pairing, though Manning had sanctioned it. She squeezed her eyes closed to hunt for a remedy. Short of taking on the entire float herself, she couldn't find one. Erosion banks might be aptly named, given the set-up. By the time she opened her eyes, she'd missed Manning's entire discourse on water rescue training. Good, she had opted out already.

~

Every other step creaked underfoot as Kemp escorted Delayne to his upstairs apartment for dinner. The carry-out steamed rice warmed his hands right through the bag and offset some of his worries. He could have spent a little more time in cleanup mode earlier, but the bell had rung in the clinic announcing a walk-in customer.

"I can't believe I forgot the plum sauce." She swiped her bangs to one side and waited for him to open the door. "This duck sauce I picked up won't be quite the same."

"No worries. I'm not a picky eater, as you're finding out. Welcome to my humble abode." He turned the knob and hesitated. "Just as a caveat, I rented the clinic space before I knew this came with it."

"Let me in, Kemp. I'm not here to judge you by where you live."

"Or how I live? What a relief." He chuckled and

pushed the door open. "It's not the stone ranch house at Lost Creek, that's for sure."

Delayne passed him and wandered toward the kitchen, stopping to place the puppy on the worn hardwood floor. "Bring that carry-out over here so I can start the fried rice. You got the frozen peas and carrots, right?"

He took a peek in the bag. "Check and check. Here is the steamed rice and what looks like a hundred packets of duck sauce."

"Well, those eggrolls might not be as good the second time around—so they'll need lots of sauce. Do you have a frying pan around here?" She started to swing her purse in a wide arc, but cushioned the landing at the last second. With an extraction straight out of a bomb disarmament manual, she lowered her fingertips into a side compartment and lifted out an egg. "Here it is—the secret ingredient of fried rice."

Kemp had begun a dutiful search for the frying pan and glanced up to witness her precious egg. "Hang on. I think the pan is down here." Once he'd slid the oven drawer open, he spotted a stick-proof pan. He lifted it to show her as the puppy ran up his back for a mountain-climbing exercise.

"No Strappy. Down boy." Delayne bent to corral the little imp, causing the egg to roll out of its protective napkin and hurtle toward the floor.

In one fell swoop, Kemp leveled the pan under the egg and netted it like a fish falling over the side of a boat. It cracked on impact.

She deposited the dog back in the living room and headed for the sink. "Don't dump that out. I can work with it."

"Let's call it a head start." He placed the pan onto the burner.

The water splashed in the sink. "Why don't you tackle the eggrolls, and let me cook the fried rice?" She wrung the excess water from her hands.

"Okay. How do you want them?"

"Line them up on a cookie sheet for the oven. That will keep the wrappers crisp."

He snapped his fingers and opened the side cabinet. This time he knew the territory, as he had heated up some frozen pizza on it before. His menu had certainly improved as of late. After laying out the pan, he dodged Delayne to get to the fridge. "So, anything new at work?"

"Hold on. I need cooking oil or butter."

"One tub of not-quite-butter, coming right up. I have some news for you—but I want you to go first." He handed over the cooking lubricant and studied her as she picked out the last fragments of eggshell.

"There's a new girl in resource management, a grad student from the university named Eva Norton. She landed a two-year grant to document erosion banks along the river. Get this—she plans to float the entire length in the next few weeks while the water levels are adequate." She switched on the front burner.

Kemp tried to align the third eggroll, but it had a mind of its own. "The erosion bank study sounds interesting. I think we spotted a couple of bare banks near Pruitt."

"Manning recruited volunteers to help with the float. Guess who took the upper river?" She waggled her eyebrows.

"You did, naturally." Two more eggrolls joined the

Legion of Honor lined up at attention on the pan.

"Well, I felt sorry for her—and there were no other females at the staff meeting. For midriver, Timber volunteered, but it's the lower river pairing that still has me concerned."

"You don't trust an intern?" He leveled the second row to match the first, six soldiers per line, all volunteering for oven duty.

"Tommy Lee volunteered for lower river. I'd forgotten they stationed him down there. So Manning sanctioned it, but I didn't like the look on Tommy Lee's face. Did I mention? Eva looks like she's going on seventeen."

"But canoeing should be safe enough." He brought the pan to her, hopeful for a commendation.

Her brow furrowed instead. "That's continuous days of canoeing—with nights camped out on river rock. Most of the lower river lacks access. How's that for throwing your lamb to the wolves?" She switched the oven dial to pre-heat and took the pan. "Nice spacing here, Doc."

He howled in response. The melted butter began to sizzle against the edge of the broken egg. He fished out a spatula and handed it to her. "Oh, I saved some dessert for you—from my outing today to visit the popcorn lady."

"Really? Let me taste some. Is it caramel corn?" She scrambled the egg yolk and looked up at him. "Toss the peas and carrots into the microwave for a couple of minutes."

"No, it's cinnamon corn, the current summer front-runner. I can vouch for its ranking—good stuff." He dropped the poly bag into the microwave and set the knob. The turntable started spinning, accompanied by a hum. "And get this. The popcorn lady, Liv, has a niece in Western Grove who wants to bring her mobile dog wash business into Harrison one day a week. She needs a hook-up location, so I'm considering the clinic."

"Wow, she could at least help you pay rent, right? What would it cost you—a little water?"

"And maybe some inconvenience. But the added exposure would offset that, as dogs would be coming and going all day. I could run a special for heartworm treatments and required vaccinations, trying to pick up some customers that way." He fidgeted with the carry-out box and managed to get the top open.

"What are you thinking? Do you want to try a flat rate or a commission based on her sales? Have you researched it online yet?"

"No. I haven't had a minute, as I got the advertising postcard set up this afternoon. One thing at a time, I guess." He pushed the rice toward her pan as the variables began to cloud his mind. Some deeper wisdom weighing in at this point would be nice. "What I'd really like to do is talk it over with my mentor. Surely in all his years of practice, he's had the occasion to share a business venture or two."

Delayne slammed down the spatula. She dumped the rice in with both hands and turned to him. "Kemp, let's talk about this for a second. I never want there to be any secrets between us, okay? I mean, we're still discovering things about one another, but I don't want to hold certain things back. Don't you agree?"

The pan crackled, so he picked up the spatula and mixed the rice into the egg. *What in the world had set off her earnestness button?* The microwave dinged, and he stepped over to retrieve the vegetables. "Honesty is always best in my book. I'm a straightforward kind of guy. For instance, I'd like to tell you to stir the pan while I add this, okay?"

"Drain it over the sink first. I'll season the rice and turn the burner down until the flavors meld." As promised, she shook the salt over the mound and gave the dish a quick stir. In seconds, she whipped out her phone and punched up a number.

Kemp tore the bag open and dodged a plume of steam. After he tipped the bag, a tiny stream of carrot-stained water leaked out. He'd give her these final ingredients, but beyond that, he didn't have a clue.

She cupped the phone against her cheek. "Hi, Daddy. How are you today?"

He stole the spatula and attempted to work the vegetables in. Space soon ran out inside the pan. Thinking the mixture looked pale, he reached for a packet of soy sauce.

"That's great," she replied. "I'm actually in the middle of cooking dinner, but I have someone who needs to talk to you about a possible business venture for his animal clinic. Hold on a second." She clamped the phone to her shoulder and took the soy sauce.

Kemp stood slack-jawed, staring into her eyes.

"No secrets," she said. "Doctor Gaylord Davidson of Eustace Springs Animal Clinic is my father. Now, talk to him about the dog wash thing. He works with a local groomer, so he'll have plenty of sound advice."

Somewhere in the process of acquiring her phone, sheer gratitude eclipsed wonderment. When she raised a brow, he brushed a kiss onto her cheek. He had been grasping at straws for success, but now he held a substantial one. The Lord sure worked in mysterious ways.

Chapter 9

Two Airedales trotted up the sidewalk toward Kemp along the makeshift corridor. If he had wondered whether the city had a considerable canine population, this holiday Monday sure proved it out. The morning had been absolutely dog-gone crazy.

He shot a finger up to cue the owner, a barrel-chested older man, to halt. Not that he needed to examine the pair, but the basset hound hadn't finished getting his ears washed out, so there was currently no room in the scrub-a-dub tub. He ran a hand down the back of the closest dog. "Are these two the same age?"

"Sisters from the same litter."

He gave the dog a pat. "This girl is running on the lean side. You have them up to date on their heartworm treatment, right?" He stood and dusted his palms off as the dogs sniffed the sidewalk. They both sported identical collars and leashes.

"The wife does the medicating. You'd have to ask her, I suppose." His salt-and-pepper mustache twitched as though to let the blame slide off.

Kemp overheard the dog washer announce the hound's final rinse. Once glance at Delayne revealed two more mini-customers joining the cue—apricot toy poodles. Eleven o'clock must have been designated their curly dog hour. His focus shifted back to the lean Airedale. "Sir, unless there's a difference in their exercise regime or food rations, I suspect this girl might have missed her dosage."

"What?" The owner seemed aghast at the possibility.

Trained to notice, he had to persist, though thin ice lay below. "Your wife may be getting the dogs mixed up. They closely favor one another, so here's what I suggest. Give the thin sister here a new red collar and keep the heavier sibling in blue. That'll help your wife keep track of who's been medicated, and each dog will get the treatment it's due."

A wave of recognition washed over the man's expression. The dogs pulled him forward a step as the basset hound vacated the wash zone. "Well, there have been some recollection issues on her part lately. No need for the dogs to suffer, though."

"Right. No need at all," Kemp replied. He offered his hand, and the man shook it looking relieved.

Becca, the animated Pails & Tails proprietor, stepped up beside him. "Who brought me two beautiful gal-pals today?" Her tone sounded cheery, especially for someone drenched head-to-toe.

"This lucky man," Kemp replied with a wink. He gave the owner a reassuring pat on the shoulder and headed for the payment table. On the way, he dodged the toy poodles whose tongues were dangling.

Noontime approached, but the sidewalk had already heated up. At least Delayne had shade under the canopy. He'd check on the rabies shot supply and chat a minute. "Hey, money lady. Do you need a break?" He tapped her sunglasses down the bridge of her nose to enjoy her lovely hazel eyes. Today, they were the color of luscious moss.

"Not me, but Strappy might benefit from a nap inside where it's cool. We need more flea and tick treatment packs anyway. Please bring some back when you return." She poked the human end of a braided leash at him.

Kemp glanced back in time to see the next customer approach, a silky Maltese. He shifted to the side of the table and took an evaluative look. The owner read the sign and began to rummage in her purse. A wash or a rabies shot, which would she want?

Delayne cleared her throat. "Conjunctivitis…kind of contagious for the wash zone, right Doctor Junkowski?"

He stepped between them and gestured to the clinic door. "Ma'am, if you would humor me a moment. It looks like your pet may have an eye problem. Since it's contagious by contact, we'd better be proactive in getting it properly treated."

"Oh, my word. I've already wiped his eyes once this morning. I should have known that something was up. Can you treat it?" She dropped her wallet back in her purse, her brow knit with concern.

"You bet, as easy as eye drops, though it would make the doggie wash off limits today, if you don't mind. Come right inside." He stepped toward the clinic door when the braided leash appeared over the table. He reached back, grabbed it, and gave the pup a whistle. With the additional dog, the trek indoors became quite a promenade. The air conditioning soon made the exodus worthwhile.

As he passed the front counter, a glimpse at the calendar reminded him next month's rent was due. The Maltese represented his third clinical treatment of the morning. Maybe he wouldn't have to dip into savings for the rent this month, a real first. "Please wait for me in the exam room there. I'll crate this little fellow for his midday nap and be right in with the eye drops."

"Thank you, doctor. I'm relieved for your expedient attention to Bailey here."

Kemp walked to the back, pressed a kiss onto Strappy's head, and lowered the pup into its crate for safekeeping. The water bowl sloshed and the pup went right for it. After clipping the crate shut, he ventured to the dispensary cabinet and extracted the eye drops. He had samples of an array of products, thanks to his pharmaceutical rep college friend. The time had come to make something out of nothing, including a rent payment for his monthly brick-and-mortar existence.

~

Delayne knew lunchtime had arrived without looking at her phone. She stretched her legs under the table and tried to block out the aroma of fried onions from somewhere up the street. The parade of dirty pooches had been steady all morning. Whatever deal Kemp had arranged with Pails & Tails would pay dividends by the end of the day. Good for him. He sure needed it.

She broadened her focus to people watch during the spare moment. A young couple across the street caught her attention. When the girl gave a mild protest and pulled away from an embrace, she spotted Tommy Lee. *Interesting.* What kind of woman was he attracted to when he wasn't using force? Or at least, using more charm than force.

The lean girl backed away from him with a playful laugh, a tattoo gleaming from her bare shoulder. As they walked on, Tommy Lee managed to trap her with his arm. She stole his hat in return, which led to a lengthy kiss.

Repulsed at the public display of affection, Delayne turned to gain a new perspective and found a woman standing by the canopy pole. "Hi there. Can I help you? This is the doggie wash booth, but I see you don't have any canine friend with you today."

"No, I'm Liv, the popcorn lady. I managed to get away from my shop to check on my niece, Becca. How's business been this morning?"

"Non-stop like a train station. Believe me, lots of satisfied customers have left that tub. The weather couldn't have been more cooperative today. She's even had to restrain a couple of kids who wanted some heat relief in the hose spray."

She laughed, her gray eyes sparkling. "Becca has wanted a presence here in Harrison for awhile. It looks like the wait was well worth it. Maybe the link with 'Cures for Canines' worked to her advantage." Someone whistled and she gave an energetic wave toward the wash station.

"Doctor Junkowski is inside right now treating a Maltese. I know he'd like to thank you for your sample last week. I helped him with that postcard mailing, which is another reason to thank you. Great popcorn, by the way.”

“Thank God above, at least half the town seems to think so today. I’ve had to pop twice my usual amount. Not that I’m complaining. I could use a day like this once a month all summer long.”

Kemp stepped up beside her. “Me, too, Liv. I guess special events on holidays are good for business. And you were right about Becca. She *is* a real go-getter.”

The woman placed a motherly hand on his forearm. “I plan to steal her away for half an hour, so we can eat lunch together while I’ve got someone tending the store. I hope you won’t protest too much.”

“I won’t let him,” Delayne replied. “We need lunch, too. I’m heading off in the direction of that onion aroma that’s been tempting me for half an hour.”

“Aha. Bart’s Philly Steak Sandwich Hut takes yet another victim.” She laughed in a knowing way. “I’ll send some sweet popcorn back with Becca, so don’t fall for Bart’s drowned brownie. It only adds needless calories and two-fifty to your bill.”

“On behalf of ‘Cures for Canines,’ we solemnly accept your charity,” he said.

Delayne stood, restless for change. “Kemp, we’re in a lull right now. Go get that clock sign out of the clinic’s front window so we can close down shop for lunch break. You’ll need to lock the cash box away, too.”

Liv began to walk toward the doggie wash to join Becca.

“Man, I love decisive women. Let me lock up and I’ll be ready for lunch.” He slid the money box off the table and made a comical gesture at how heavy it was.

“I kept the event money separate from the doggie

wash takings, so don't worry about getting them mixed up," she added.

"With you running the table, why would I worry?" He gave her an expressive look and disappeared into the clinic.

Delayne bagged the remaining supplies and cleared the table. No use opening themselves to petty theft losses while away. She stepped to the door and popped the bag onto the chair just inside the door. When Kemp appeared from the back, lunch seemed a certainty.

"Strappy's snoring, he's so zonked out." He laughed and took her by the elbow.

She stood her ground. "Lunch is on me today, doctor. Or you'll have to find another assistant for the afternoon." She knew he'd likely balk, but had determined that one hundred percent of his earnings today should go to finance the clinic.

Kemp swished his lips over his front teeth in contemplation. "That generous offer might just thrust me into the realm of solvency for the month. Can you live with such a swollen ego?"

"Yes, but I can't live without that onion-topped sandwich for much longer. Come on, we only have half an hour." She headed out the door and noticed he didn't lag too far behind.

"I see that decisive can leak straight into bossy when a lady gets hungry." He locked the door with a turn of his wrist and passed her a little wink.

"Race you to Bart's," she said in a challenging tone. Before he could pose a dignified objection, she broke into a full-fledged run. Now he'd have to chase her, and not because she was paying today either. She tossed a wave over her shoulder and headed for onion central.

~

The afternoon grew less frantic by three o'clock, though Kemp had no fondness for slow business. A thinning crowd evidenced the start of activities at the fairground on the edge of town. The Lions Club had hosted a small carnival for part of their annual fundraiser. As much as he liked eating cotton candy and riding the Scrambler, he couldn't garner any interest to partake of the offering.

Becca walked up to the table where Delayne sat, wiping her hands on a small towel. "Hey guys, I've been thinking about Aunt Liv's suggestion about making the bank drop early. Since we're in a lull, I might go do that now. What do you think?"

Since they hadn't washed a customer or shot a flank in the last fifteen minutes, Kemp gave her a nod.

"How about I walk you over to First Freedom?" Delayne offered. "Two people are safer than one."

"I think that's a good idea," Kemp replied. "I'll stay and man the fort. Why don't you count out the money inside the clinic? Out of sight, out of mind."

"Another good idea," Delayne replied. "Where are your deposit bags, Kemp? I'll drop your takings in as well, and you can settle up with the rabies event coordinator by check. That's safer to mail anyway."

"Look on the front counter about the second cubby space. There should be four or five bags there." He dropped his gaze to the table and saw that only three rabies vaccines remained. "It would be nice to sell out today, so I'll hang around up here until four o'clock or so."

Delayne grabbed the cash box and led the way inside.

He overheard a positive remark from Becca about the clinic as the door closed. When his knee gave a wincing ache, he slid into the chair and regarded the street traffic. Only a few individuals loitered at the sales rack down the way. Two cars idled up to the traffic light down the block. An overzealous speaker drummed bass against the languid scenery. The light changed and the low rider with the excess bass rolled up the street.

Half-dazed by weary limbs, Kemp failed to recognize Tommy Lee Resnick until the customized car rolled directly in front of the clinic. The woman draped around his neck didn't stir a muscle as they passed. Deciding not to be cordial, he folded his hands on the tabletop.

Tommy Lee looked his way about the time Delayne popped out of the clinic's door with the bank bag. Before she got to the table, he shot a one-fingered salute at Kemp and drove on.

Becca made small talk as they approached the table.

Kemp's stomach churned at the sight of the reprehensible intern. Maybe he should flag him down and ask for his spare tire back. Or he could ask him to sell one of those fancy chrome tailpipes and buy him a replacement. He'd read in Psalms about the wicked seeming to prosper, but had never felt it so acutely until that moment.

Delayne lowered her glasses and looked into his eyes. Her brow rose in a questioning response to his blank stare. "So, we're off to the bank then. You're on wash duty until we return."

"Oh, no, Doctor Junk," Becca replied. "If someone comes up, try to hold them off until I can get back…Or better yet, talk them into the discount rabies shot first to kill some time."

Kemp harrumphed. "I guess it wouldn't be the first time a needle was employed to kill time. Straight to the bank deposit drawer then, and straight back."

Delayne tilted her head. "Yes, sir. We're the bee-line girls. And we're packing some heavy bags."

"That's the problem in a nutshell, little bird. Now get back here already." He folded his hands under his chin and tried to fight off a bout of sleepiness.

"No need to check on the puppy," Delayne added. "You wore him out after lunch."

"I wore us both out. Just punch me in the side if I'm asleep at my post when you get back." When he stretched out over the table, Becca giggled.

Delayne dug a fist into her hip. "At least watch us head down Second Street, Kemp."

"I've got you for approximately fifteen seconds then. One sheep walking, two sheep walking…" His voice ramped down to inaudible.

"Very funny." She turned with purpose and headed off to the bank.

After the women disappeared, he fell into a delicate place, dark and weightless. No tasks awaited here. No one stood insistent close by. It stretched before him as a neutral territory—and grew deeply quiet. He moved about with little effort, yet seemed to go nowhere.

A knock sounded and light cracked into the darkness. When he lifted his head, someone stood before him. The man's face looked somewhat familiar, though his instant recall lagged.

"Doctor Junkowski, so sorry to barge in like this, but I've got a situation that's out of control. I thought you might help us out." He gestured down by his side.

For the first time, Kemp noticed the sleek head bobbing beside the man's shorts. A long snout sniffed the table's edge and a beautiful pure-bred collie came into focus. "Of course. What seems to be the problem?" He stood and partially stumbled around the corner to get a closer look at the canine.

The man clamped a blood-stained cloth under the dog's jaw. "I'm Dave Manning from over at resource management."

"Yes, sir. I recognize you now. Want to tell me what happened?" He gestured toward the clinic and positioned behind the door to hold it open.

Manning strained against the tightened leash. "I don't really know, quite honestly. I was in the backyard when she walked by the rose bush I had just trimmed. The next thing I know, her coat is matted with blood."

"Likely a cyst burst under the thick mane. She must have raked it on a stiff stem and opened it up." He led the way to the exam room, but didn't miss the look of guilt on the man's face. "This cyst would have drained at some point, so don't let it sting you with blame. Think you can help me lift her onto the table?"

"Sure thing. I appreciate this service, it being a holiday and everything."

"Well, my clinic has been open all day because of the 'Cures for Canines' event. Things have tapered off this afternoon, but we were sure hopping earlier."

"Thank goodness for small miracles, then. You're available now, and that's the main thing." Manning wiped his forehead with his arm.

Kemp pulled the fur back and found the wound, a three-quarter-inch gash on the outside of a golf ball-sized lump. The putrid smell almost knocked him over.

"I'm going to have to drain this thing, which might require shaving off a spot here. Who am I working on, by the way?"

"This is Zenda, the queen of our family. She gets the foot of the bed, the den sofa, and everything else she wants, when she wants it. Our kids are grown, so she's all the baby Marge and I have left. Now you see why I'm in the doghouse." He tried to snicker. It came out weak.

"Let's see if I can save both of you then," Kemp replied. He grabbed a local anesthetic and placed the bottle on the table close by. "You'll have to hold her in place as best as you can, leash and everything. I'll shave a swath and get the local going."

"Got it. You'd think I would have noticed something walnut-sized before now."

"Don't knock yourself out over it. She's a real beauty, all right. I've never seen a collie in a summer haircut, but you might give it some thought for heat relief." He placed the razor on the dog's throat and worked around the gash in rapid strokes. The blade caked up and had to be wiped repeatedly, but he handled it. Getting the gauze pad soaked with anesthetic was more of an art. Soon, he had the site prepped and stood ready to drain the abscess.

Manning mumbled some words of comfort to the old dog and stroked her back.

"Here comes the pressure, Dave. You've got to hold Zenda with both hands for me, or she'll come off the table."

"You bet, Doc." He leaned over the dog and trapped it along its entire length.

Kemp reached for a scraping tool with a shallow

bowl at its tip. With a drawn breath, he set to work clearing the wound. Under the dog's thrashing, he somehow missed the sound of the clinic door opening. Footsteps approached the exam room.

"You-whoo. Are you asleep at the job?" Delayne called.

Manning's head flew up at the sound of her voice.

Kemp straightened, knowing help had arrived. "I'm elbow deep. Come wash up and assist me, will you?"

Her eyes widened as she stepped into the small room. The collie attempted to get on its feet, but Manning immediately recovered his grip.

Blood covered the burnished tabletop. The faucet turned on behind him as he attempted a swipe at the back of the wound. So pustulated, he could barely see what he was touching.

Delayne's ponytail brushed his arm. "May I suggest a saline rinse?"

"Yes, please," Kemp replied. "I'll hold the cyst open."

She returned in seconds with a narrow-necked squeeze bottle. "Becca wants to stay until five, by the way. She'll run the front until we can get back out there." A thin jet began to wash the sore.

"I'm really sorry about this." Manning hung his head.

"Not at all. This is why Kemp came to Harrison, sir. So our animals could have better care. Your collie is in capable hands."

Kemp continued to scrape out the cyst, ever conscious of Delayne's close presence. He'd never had anyone he could count on to assist before. Beyond relieving, it felt incredible. He collected a large mass of pustulated tissue and deposited it in a small tray. "Be sure to rinse this side. I'll hold it open."

The dog objected with a twitch, but was no match for three against one. Once Delayne finished the rinse, he assessed the jagged-edged opening. "I'd better close this with a stitch or three."

Delayne seemed already ahead of him with her acute sense of purpose. "Where's the suture set?"

"Top left drawer. A medium needle, please." He bumped Manning's shoulder with his and tipped his chin toward Delayne over his shoulder.

Manning gave him a knowing look, his pale face regaining a bit of color.

"Almost done here. Nine times out of ten, the cyst reabsorbs and the trouble goes into the history books."

"I'll take those odds. It seems like summer's come out of the chute with a pistol in both hands. What an opening rampage."

Delayne approached and offered the needle. "You're letting that chronic motor pool theft get under your skin, boss man." Her calm tone soothed over the troubled topic.

Kemp motioned for the synthetic gut and soon had the first stitch knotted. One led to another, but the collie took the pricks like a champ. He compromised with four stitches and tugged the last one into place. Though the skin looked red and aggravated, the sore was clean. He swiped cleansing gauze over it and stood to full height. "A rose by any other name…"

"Would stink just as sweet," Manning replied. "At least I have my baby back."

"Yes, praise God and thank Doctor Junkowski," Delayne added with a blossoming smile. "Now, can I talk you into a doggie wash to get her cleaned up? We're having a special today and Becca can fix you right up."

Manning stroked the dog lovingly between the ears. "Well, that would give me time to clean up my car."

"Perfect. I'll walk you out there," she replied.

"Let's get Zenda back on the floor then." Kemp gestured to the dog's hind quarters and Manning shifted back. Together they heaved the big dog off the table. Its tail soon made a slow wag. "See, a happy customer."

"You sure turned that catastrophe around for me, Doc. Much obliged for that."

Kemp nodded and smiled. "Let me clean up and I'll come help you with the car."

Delayne led the way to the doggie wash, but Manning hesitated at the exam room door. "You've already done enough, Doctor Junkowski. If you'll loan me some rags, I'll get the rest."

Kemp washed his hands up to his elbows and considered the opportunity. By all accounts, he was one spare tire and a GPS unit away from being fully done. He had Manning's undivided attention standing on neutral territory. Whatever the motor pool issue, he wanted to add his two cents, and maybe link a name to it, to boot. "I'll help you," he replied. "I want to."

~

Delayne shifted closer under Kemp's arm and propped her feet up on the coffee table. Though his eyes were closed, he still seemed to be enjoying her company. Her pre-dawn survey came to mind, but she trapped the moan it regularly solicited as of late. It was almost as if Ross Connors was trying to keep her wandering out there instead of pinpointing prime grouse habitat. She could take on the mapping task instead, but Connors had been brought in as an expert consultant. Manning would demand a better explanation than a gripe about the rough terrain.

"You were quite the assistant this afternoon." Kemp's lips parted in a lazy smile, but his eyes remained closed. "That came off as nothing short of amazing to me. I needed the help and there you were, administering it with expertise. Should I thank your father for that training?"

"Yes, his answer to my 'I'm bored' comments was to keep me busy in the animal hospital. Since the dogs and cats were adorable for the most part, I couldn't say no."

"Were you ever interested in becoming an animal doctor to follow in his footsteps?"

"No way." She leaned her head back on his arm. "Give me the great outdoors. Dad has to stay in that office every hour the hospital's open, unless he does a farm visit."

"I didn't know he did large animals, too. Guess I need to meet this guy and learn more about him. I am dating his daughter, after all."

She looked at him to see how serious he was. Tiny amber slits paid her back for the examination. "Maybe you two could go fishing out behind our house. That's where he solves all the major issues facing humankind."

"Hmmm, I like the sound of that, almost as much as canoeing the Buffalo with you."

"No, I have a new partner, remember? Eva and I are due to start the upper river this Wednesday. After three days of paddling, you may have to recreate on the water without me."

"Where's the fun in that?" He clamped her neck in the crook of his elbow and drew her closer. "I can't believe you're trading me in for some Garden of Eva nature photographer."

"But you can have Daddy. I was planning to go home this coming weekend, in fact. I'll do my laundry and you can fish. I promise to cook whatever you two catch. Is that appealing?"

"Are you kidding? Food, fun, and fishing. What's not to like? What about the pup?"

"Yes, Strappy gets to ride shotgun. Daddy hasn't even seen him yet."

"Don't make me fight him over veterinarian custody rights. I already have dibs."

Her ear tingled with his nearness. "Yes, you have dibs, Doctor Junkowski. Does that mean I can count you in for the trip home Saturday?"

"Yes, count me in. Now, I need to send you home, so you can chase your grouse in the morning. Maybe Chinstrap needs to stay with me tonight. You can pick him up after work."

He traced her jawline with his fingertip.

"What? I'm lonesome just at the thought of it." Reactive, she almost jerked out of his grasp. When his long lashes fluttered open at the disturbance, his amber eyes held nothing but affection, all focused on her.

"Let's not talk about lonesome, Layne." He placed a kiss on her lips and pulled her closer to adjust his angle. "Not when we have tomorrow."

"And the next tomorrow," she added. When he came to say goodnight, she slid her arms around his neck. Maybe if she held on tight, the tender moment would last. She could replay that sequence all the way back to Lost Creek. Their second kiss fell like the down of a thistle lofted by a gentle breeze. *Mercy me*. A girl could get used to something like that.

Chapter 10

You have got to be kidding me. Delayne ran her fingers through the outer pocket of her field pack until they showed through the unraveled bottom seam. She'd noticed the small tear last week, but shrugged it off. Dating left little free time for upkeep, so something like mending was out of the question—which left her here—without a route map.

She gritted her teeth and mentally retraced the data she'd added earlier. Pursuit of a faint drumming sound led to the direct sighting of two male grouse, a heady pre-dawn encounter, especially given the lateness in mating season. She could readily mark that upper elevation location again using the master map back in the resource management office.

Her main problem involved where to head from here. She knelt along the rock ledge that outcropped off the slope. On every survey route she'd walked, *down* meant *out*. With Connors running her into increasingly marginal habitat, she'd gained more shear rock face. So *down* didn't come easy and *out* wouldn't be immediate. Plus, Connors would gloat when she recorded the new drumming log location. *Of all the luck.*

She paused on the unforgiving rock and studied the shadows cast by the tallest trees. Still morning, the shadows pointed west. She needed to head west. From this particular site, that involved a twenty-five-foot vertical drop. Apprehensive of taking on that length of a drop, she decided to scout the ledge for any manner of stair-step climb down—anything that might break up the death-wish descent below her.

Only when she stood did she realize how far up the jagged Ozark landscape she had ventured. Hardwood trees had become outnumbered by the evergreens. The grouse species preferred hardwoods for cover. Therefore, so did she. Toeing the edge of the rock ledge, she glanced down its length. It looked hopeless.

Somewhere along her steep-edged route, she remembered to take her troubles to the Lord. She never walked alone when she walked with God. Maybe she should even consider herself closer to his heavenly throne room at this altitude. When she tried to pray aloud, it came out like a mumble. She halted, clinched her fists to her temples, and squeezed her eyes closed. "Help me, God. Get me out of here."

In a matter of seconds, a descent route appeared on the ledge ahead. Three substantial steps lowered to leave a final drop of less than ten feet. Elated, Delayne centered the weight of her pack and set a new strategy. She would front the rock and lead with her right foot. That would put her back on her dominant foot to make the final drop.

As she eased over the edge, the rock crumbled

against her ribs. Loosened chunks cascaded below. Maybe she should take this slower, as the rock seemed more weathered than she had anticipated. Her right foot landed solid on the shelf and she gained the first five feet. She paused for a breath and studied the next platform.

Ragged-edged and slightly slanted, the second step-down would bring her five more feet. The third step sat immediately below, possibly only three or four feet lower. With those under her belt, she could stretch out her full length and make the final drop. "Feet don't fail me now," she said in jest. She licked her lips. They were chapped beyond belief.

Delayne made the transition from a seated position, opting at the last second to make landfall with both feet. After clearing her pack, she eased from the shelf and went momentarily airborne. When her left foot struck, it took out half the second shelf. Her right foot only made partial contact and slipped completely off. For a harsh second, she stood on mountain air. Then she tumbled.

Knowing the third shelf remained below she attempted to get her feet under her, but ran out of real estate. Striking shin-first along its weathered edge, she careened off sideways, cringing in pain. The ten foot drop transpired without mercy. She managed to grab the pack by a strap and tuck it under her chin, then braced for impact.

The surface of the land below had hardened over eons of exposure. Her left foot touched down first. Her knee buckled on contact. A white-hot flash shot up her leg as she landed on her left hip. Her head whiplashed, but lodged into the pack for a relatively soft impact. The breath she'd been holding midair fled the scene, lending the sensation of being flattened side-to-side.

Now as low as she could go, she attempted to raise her head. Responding to the angry throb from her left hip, she pushed off with her foot to roll over. Pain knifed up her trunk and her head began to spin. In seconds, white-hot pain merged into a jet-black tunnel where everything went limp and painless.

~

Kemp maximized his last working hour by packing up his payment to "Cures for Canines" so it would be a done deal. He opted for keeping the remaining two vaccines and included the discounted compensation for them. Evaluative, he determined the exposure in the community had been well worth the effort. Plus, it had given them a focal point for launching the new doggie wash to Harrison, a real financial boost for his day.

As he reinforced the envelope's seal with a length of tape, the front door chime sounded. He looked up to see a familiar face. "Good afternoon, Mr. Manning. How's our favorite collie doing today?"

A glimmer of positive reaction rippled across his steely expression. "Much better, Doc. Thanks for asking. I've come about another matter."

Kemp read the man's stiff posture and put down the envelope. "What's up then?"

"I came over because I know you and Delayne are close. She's…well…she's overdue from coming in from the field today."

The hairs on the back of his neck began to stand up. If anyone knew how to keep a schedule, Delayne did. "She didn't mention any extra errands to me last night. In fact, I was expecting her within the hour to pick up her speckled mutt."

Manning wiped a hand over his mouth and glanced up at the wall clock. "I have to make a decision whether to go scout for her, in case something happened. We need daylight, so we have until eight-thirty or so. Quite honestly, I need your help. I asked Connors to double up with me, but he had a lodge meeting where he's presenting the program tonight, so he bowed out."

A bitter taste came into Kemp's mouth, but he decided not to express the barb regarding Connors lack of cooperation. He'd bide his time on that one. One look at the appointment book told him nothing held him at the clinic. "I'm your man then. Give me a second to close up shop here. I'll crate the puppy since we don't know how long we'll be."

"Meet me out front then," Manning replied. "I brought a four-wheel drive truck. She's way up in Ponca, so we'll need it."

Kemp nodded as he walked toward the back. The puppy trotted to his side, so he scooped it up and headed for the crate. "Sorry, buddy. Ladies first today. In you go." He refilled the food dish before securing the door. A glance at his dress shoes reminded him that he had something more appropriate for the rugged terrain. Headed upstairs with long bounds, he grabbed his jeans as thoughts of Delayne filtered into his rationale. "Hang in there, little bird," he whispered. Dread clouded his next thought—a scouring mental blast of nonstop dread.

~

Dehydrated and uncomfortable to the point of growing stiff, Delayne examined her progress, which amounted to dragging her body into the shade of a rangy cedar tree. Her left knee failed to hold any weight, so she could only hop for short distances or scoot on her bottom. Neither offered adequate methods for navigating the woodlands. Her stomach growled.

Down to a solitary granola bar, she rummaged in her pack and produced it. Now her dinner would match her lunch, an oatmeal-encrusted plank that would keep her alive through the night. Unfortunately, its dry texture would demand another sip of water, her other limited resource. Her immediate future began to play out like an ecology lesson gone amuck. She wanted homeostasis back, a balanced state where she had everything she needed in life.

So busy managing the pain in her left knee and hip, she hadn't allowed her mind to wander toward the personal comfort zone. Strappy came to mind in a weak moment. The playful pup entertained her for the briefest of seconds, and then generated a longing straight from the heart. When Kemp's brown eyes joined the imaginary parade, she sobbed. They were both together, but where was she? Stranded here adding to the duff layer in a forest that didn't care.

For the first time in a long time, she reexamined her fieldwork career strategy. By thirty years of age, most field biologists tended to gravitate to office jobs. As they advanced, less time in the field became a tradeoff for more office responsibilities. She had yet to reach that fulcrum-point, but had never given it much thought before now. Thirty was not that far off.

She exhaled and relaxed back on the pack. Its padding reminded her that the rain slicker inside would have to double as her blanket tonight. Her cell phone now bore a cracked faceplate and seemed inoperable, or at minimum, out of the service area. No, she had literally fallen off the face of the earth today. One question remained. Would anyone notice?

~

Kemp should have been relieved when Manning spotted Delayne's truck, but the knot in his stomach only grew bigger. He glanced up the immediate hillside and could barely distinguish what she had been referring to as the old logging road. Trees with girths larger than his thighs now rose from the rutted terrain, evidencing the passage of a considerable amount of time. He slid from the truck as Manning made a phone call to report the truck had been located.

For the first time, he spotted the rock climbing gear stowed in back. He'd not given a single thought of having to broach rough terrain to bring Delayne back. He let out a slow exhale that bore a whistle on the end. Maybe he'd tie the top laces of his hiking boots as he waited. When he bent down for the adjustment, his temples started to throb and his backpack shifted.

The truck door slammed. "We'll take the minimum for now, a lowering rope," Manning said. "I went heavy with all this rescue gear. Hope my Boy Scout tendencies didn't throw you."

"Well, sir. I'm a positive thinker, so I imagined her in some picnic-like setting having just forgotten the time."

"That would be a rose-colored, bottom-of-the-hill assessment. By the way, out here, I'm just Dave. You've got your phone, right? In case we get separated, you'll need it." He grabbed a coiled rope and began to walk up the road, testing her truck door as he went by. It was locked.

Kemp trotted a few steps to catch up. "Yes, I've got my phone, a bottle of water, my first aid kit, and extra gauze for excessive bleeding, in case I'm on a large animal call."

Manning gave a slight grin. "Turns out you're the right man to team with for a rescue, after all. Besides, Connors bores me to tears in the field with his inane need to point out every sprig of poison ivy occurring along the way."

Kemp seized the mention, thinking the hike up would provide the perfect neutral setting for disclosure. "You knew Delayne was having some differences with him regarding these field routes, right?"

Manning's brow knit. "What do you mean?"

"She told me she felt the upper elevations were marginal as far as suitable habitat. The terrain up there had become nearly impassable. She talked about having to make drops off of ledges more than once to maintain the route. I know she's capable in the field, so I kept my nose out of it, but now I wished I hadn't." He stumbled over loose rocks in the rut and decided to walk off to one side.

Manning held his peace for about twenty-five yards as they ascended. He heaved the rope over one shoulder and finally gave Kemp a prolonged stare. "Delayne truly is masterful at what she has accomplished up here. I think you'll be impressed. I gave her lots of room to operate, as she has seniority over the typical intern we get. Her grant runs out the end of June and I've been searching everywhere to find funding to keep her on staff."

"I'm sure she appreciates the vote of confidence on your part, Dave. She's actually looking forward to this canoe trip with the photographer, since her research is winding down."

"Is she? Then I should have her assist with the whole trip downriver. Eva could stand the capable support, and it would keep me from having to rely on those dunderhead interns on the lower river. Hey, watch your footing as the slope steepens through here."

No sooner had the warning been issued when Kemp stumbled on a tree root. He threw his arms out for balance and caught himself before his knees hit the ground, a last-minute save.

"See? When you add rocks to the terrain, nothing's a safe bet." Manning pointed to a stand of trees ahead. "We're coming up on her first section. It contains three drumming logs. The grouse population is going crazy down here."

"That's good, isn't it? For a restocked population, I mean." Kemp shrugged his shoulders to get his backpack into a more comfortable position.

"After thirty years of re-introduction, yes, the population is thriving. Extirpation isn't the kind of natural heritage I take pride in, as a native of Arkansas. We should have been more conscious of the need for species conservation as part of our wildlife management. But back in the day, game species were treated differently, because hunters didn't want limits on their sport. It proved to be a short-sighted mentality."

Kemp glanced up the hill and found the terrain largely unaffected by the forces of civilized man. Even the logging road ruts had naturalized. "Was the saving grace the land itself? This habitat looks untouched to me—and hopefully to the grouse."

"Yes, the ruggedness of the terrain here saved the native vegetative cover, which lent great habitat for the restocking effort. We curse the rocks when we should bless them. They do more than protect this backwoods way of life."

Kemp nodded and walked ahead. The trees all seemed to be of similar age, probably evidence that the loggers had taken out the larger specimen. Tranquility wrapped the hill as birds darted from close-by trees, threatened by their presence. No wonder Delayne wanted to spend time up here. It more than offset the office arguments and lab time getting the map done.

When the wind blew through a slight clearing in the canopy, he noticed something flapping from the trunk of a nearby hardwood tree. He stepped closer and found a metal-clad circle bearing triple letters and a solitary number.

"That's Delayne's system for numbering the routes. Any other researcher can come behind her using the maps and locate each drumming log to check for activity in years to come. It's a baseline that will be fundamental to the species upkeep decades from now."

"Everyone should leave such a high mark on their work," he agreed, fingering the tag. Having shielded his personal reaction from the time Manning had entered the clinic, he could now release a bit of that angst and allow himself to think about Delayne. In short, he was proud of her. He tried not to let his thoughts drift to what she'd be doing once her grant ran its course. That would defeat all she had accomplished while here, and he couldn't allow that progression.

Manning passed by, focused on the route ahead. "We're looking for the marker 'UND dash seven.' I checked her master map before coming out. That's next in line."

"You mean, assuming she made it to the start of the route and posted the marker, right?"

"She made it," Manning replied, not bothering to look up.

"When we get to this 'UND' series, we should start calling out to her, in case she got off the trail or something." Kemp gestured to both sides, thinking the woodland was fairly expansive.

"Good technique. Let's make a note to watch for that first marker then, and anything else that seems out of the ordinary."

Kemp pressed on is silence for the next twenty minutes. The fact that Delayne hadn't called in bothered him the most. Now that he saw the terrain up-close, he wished they had implemented a better verification system for her remote field work. He'd tuck the idea away and mention it later. At least twenty years his senior, Manning had fallen behind his pace.

A marker came up on his left and he checked it with a quick glance, not wanting to slow down yet. The letters "UND" burned into focus and he halted midstride. The woods seemed different here, and there weren't as many rotting logs lying around. Maybe Delayne had coded the "UND" for "undesirable" as a jab at Connors' flawed judgment. It made him smile to even consider it. When Manning huffed up, Kemp held up the marker to show him.

"Okay. We'd better start the shout-outs. Want me to go first?"

"No, sir. I've been saving up for this one, so stand back and let me at it." He stiff-armed the resource manager back in courtesy and waited for him to gain a few steps. "De-lay-ne," he called at the top of his lungs.

"Where are you?"

Only the rocks answered, and they weren't highly informative.

Manning paused for a good ten seconds before he trudged on. "I'll take number two." He switched the rope onto his other shoulder and scanned the east side of the logging road.

The silence birthed a bit of dread for Kemp, as he hadn't anticipated the void of habitability that the rugged landscape held. In a burst of movement, a small lizard scrambled into a crack in the rocks by his feet. Even that reptilian sign of life didn't reassure him this place was livable. The lower elevations probably told a different story, and he could only hope Delayne would have made her way down sufficiently to gain more signs of life. He mulled it over, but before he knew it, Manning was shouting her name at marker number two. After a pause, he proceeded upslope.

A fishbone seemed to stick in his throat around marker number six, as their systematic efforts seemed foiled by the vastness of the craggy hillside. An even number, Manning made the call. Kemp listened until he thought his eardrum would shatter under the pressure of dead silence. Things began to get dire as the sun had slipped below the tallest trees and shadows mottled the landscape.

He removed his sunglasses and tucked them onto his hat brim. Right away, some white debris flailing in the wind snagged his attention. He made his way toward it and plucked it from a waxy-leafed shrub. With the unfolding of a single seam, it became apparent he held a map. "Hey, Dave. I think I may have found something here along survey route six." He walked toward his search partner and unfolded the map to its entirety. The name "Davidson" was printed along the top margin.

Manning took the map in hand and studied its contents. A smile crept across his face. "She located a drumming log this morning and sighted two males. I'd bet they were trying to expand their breeding territory."

"I'm thinking the girl grouse might not like it up here," he quipped. "But I doubt Delayne would let this map slip out of her clutches under normal conditions. We don't know how far the wind has blown this thing, but we can't be far off. I'm jogging up to number seven and will give the shout-out while I wait for you to catch up."

"Go ahead." Manning huffed for his next breath. "The temperature is starting to drop."

With a fire lit inside, his legs carried the flame to the upper hillside. In minutes, he located the next survey marker. He wanted this yell to be heard a country mile away, so he cupped his hands to his mouth as he studied the terrain. A break in the solid rock face opened to the west, so he aimed for it and gave it his all. "De-lay-ne?" He swallowed to lubricate his throat and his ears popped. In the clarity of the moment, he heard a faint sound like a bird calling back to him. His heart skipped a beat.

Manning came up beside him, his expression questioning.

"I think I heard something through the west break there." Kemp indicated the direction and began to head that way.

"Let's stay together from here on out," Manning insisted. "There's no time for one of us to go missing."

"Right. I'll lead and repeat the call in a short distance. Maybe she can meet us halfway." Convinced they were on the verge of a reunion, Kempt allowed optimism to buoy his spirits.

"Don't count on it," Manning replied in a low voice.

Shrugging off caution to expedite the rescue, he headed up the slope until he came to an abrupt ledge. Not expecting to confront this old foe, Kemp's vision began to spin. He crouched and took his head in his hands.

Manning soon stooped beside him. "Is it the altitude, Doc?"

"Something like that. I have an aversion to ledges...and the helpless feeling of stepping over the edge."

"Who doesn't? Let me give the call this time. Close your eyes and listen." He stood and turned his back. "Delayne Davidson...where are you?" The call echoed against the hard rock.

With his eyes squeezed shut, Kemp imagined a level place that held no threat. In the quiet, his pulse settled. His breathing soon grew regular.

"Here I am," a weak voice called from afar. "Down below the ledges."

Manning grabbed his shoulders and helped him to his feet. He laughed and shook the map at the sky. "We're onto something now, partner. Let's find a way to get down there. It looks like the hill tapers off to the west. Once we take off some of this elevation, we may be able to get to her."

"Roger that. I want to let her know we heard her, so give me the next shout-out." Kemp came off the ledge and found solid substrate to tread.

"It's all yours, Doc. Just watch your footing."

"Down is my direction. I'm good at down." He grabbed the straps and kept the backpack from beating against his frame as he descended with haste. After fifteen seconds, he spotted a rock promontory and headed for it. He had his hands cupped to his mouth before he had even arrived. "Delayne, we're on our way. Can you tell us how close we are?" He rested a palm over his skittish heart and waited for a reply as Dave caught up.

"Try one more ledge down," she replied, sounding closer this time.

"Look at that beast," Manning said, pointing to a rock formation that seemed to hang suspended in thin air.

"Something tells me I'm going to have to," Kemp replied. In no time, his tongue became glued to the roof of his mouth. He backed off the precipice and headed out to interface with the impossible. When Manning shrugged the rope off his shoulder, he stopped to hydrate his system. He started to dry heave and squelched it under a stream of tepid water. The remainder he'd save for Delayne. He just had to get to her, ledge or no ledge.

~

Tears welled in Delayne's eyes, thinking she wasn't worth all the trouble. With the assistance of a rope, Kemp scaled down the ledge that had done her in. After dropping a body length or greater, he came to her on the run. Maybe her rigged-up water bottle splint would give the knee injury away at a glance.

He landed in a swoop, took her into his arms, and

planted a kiss on her hairline. "Funny meeting you here—in the land of drumming logs."

She pressed her face into his T-shirt to bond in the reunion. "So glad you could make it."

Manning checked her leg. "It's a carry-down from here. There's no turning back."

Delayne lost herself in Kemp's amber gaze and knew, for a fact, that truth had arrived.

Chapter 11

Delayne glanced at her new roommate as she settled the bow of the canoe along the riverbank. On her sixth day with the knee injury, she had regained limited ability to use her left leg. The canoe assignment had been a saving grace, all things considered, as she got to work but didn't have to stand. At Kemp's insistence, she'd postponed the trip home over the weekend, so now she only had to get this upper river float done. "Hey Eva, don't forget the lunch cooler behind you."

The researcher turned so quick her chin-length hair flared out. "Oh, thanks. What is it with Mondays? I can't seem to get it together this morning."

"I have to stay focused," she replied, "or it costs me unnecessary steps." She lifted her braced leg into the canoe. "Sorry, I can't do the shove-off."

"No problem. I'll get us off the bank, while you get ready to paddle." Eva placed the cooler along the midrib and positioned off the bow. The camera dangling from her neck swung landward as she gave the canoe a push toward open water.

Noting the deeper green-blue water ahead, Delayne dug her paddle into the rock bottom and pried the stern into compliance. "Okay. Day Two of the upper river float is now underway."

Eva settled into her regular on-knees position in the bow. As she grabbed her paddle, she glanced over her shoulder at Delayne. "Are you comfortable enough?"

"Pretty good, actually."

"I bet you miss your puppy. I know I would." She took her first stroke off the right side.

Delayne switched the paddle to her left. A little green heron took wing from the far bank with a complaining croak. That would not embody her attitude today. "Kemp was right. The dog needs to be with him until I can walk without any pain. He'll have Strappy with him when he brings out dinner tonight, so we'll get some quality time together then. Do you want to take a minute and start the log entry for today?"

"It's narrow through here. Let me wait a few minutes and help paddle. Maybe I will after that bend up ahead." Eva turned to study the bank edge and puffed a breath through her blunt bangs. "Is it hotter today, or is it just me?"

"Oh, yeah. It's muggy all right. I'll get up some speed to cool you off."

"Hey. I forgot. Part of our lunch needs to cook. I'd better get it out."

Delayne smiled as the young researcher rummaged through the cooler and pulled out the object of her sweet-tooth vice. Soon, a full package of Oreo cookies sat on the lid, basking in the morning sun. She chuckled and took a corrective stroke. "You're not a newcomer to this neck of the woods, are you?"

"No, ma'am, and I know what I like. There's no need for hardship, just because space is limited. Tomorrow, I'm bringing my fishing pole and trolling for dinner while we float."

"That will come in handy on the overnight sections of river, for sure. Your cooler can only hold so much."

"I guess Timber can down a trout or two, given his size." She popped a visor on to keep her freckles from multiplying.

"That guy is a do-gooder, bless his soul. His mother must be a fabulous cook. We've partnered up a couple of times during training. He's pretty resourceful, all in all."

"What about Mister Good-looking from the lower river section?" Eva pivoted around to look at her. "I bet his mother isn't a fabulous cook. Ha!"

Delayne thought about the scraggly-haired country woman wearing her bathrobe outside and thinking nothing of it. "No, his maw probably has other attributes, but cooking may not be one of them. Tommy Lee doesn't come with my recommendation, either. He's trouble waiting to happen. Unpredictability is the last thing you need out on the river."

"You might be right about that. Hey, can we float closer to the east bank? If that bend isn't lined with rock, I might have my first erosion site of the day."

"Take a minute to get your logbook ready. I'll get us closer to the evidence. Hope you enjoy conducting your field research. It's always been a thrill for me."

"Absolutely. I look at it as one continuous mission of discovery." Eva surrendered her paddle and dug the waterproof bag out of the hull.

"Life's a lot like that, too," she reflected, her thoughts turning to Kemp. She had quite a bit more to discover in that realm of six-foot-four with such golden brown eyes to adore. Dinnertime couldn't come soon enough in that regard.

"Hold up," Eva insisted. "Can't you see the monster waiting over there for me?"

She raked her gaze over the embankment and a huge erosion scarp extended almost the entire outer bend. "Godzilla duly noted. Let me take some speed off before you shoot it." She dragged her paddle, which brought the nose of the canoe perpendicular to the problem.

Eva leaned over the gunwale and her camera lens soon made a series of clicks.

"Bang, bang. You're dead. I quit." Delayne laughed and righted the canoe parallel with the river's flow.

Eva looked up from the logbook to share the light moment. "If only it was that easy to kill a riverbank monster."

"Yeah, right. Then you'd be out of a research project. Up the river we go…to face the unknown foe."

"Weak poetry," Eva replied. "I'm not going to write that down." Her shoulders soon shook from muffled laughter.

"You're writing down numbers because it's a photo log, so write this down. Ten o'clock. That's when I'm going to steal and eat the first Oreo from that pack."

"Hmm. Let's see. That ratio equals four erosion scarps per cookie." Eva tapped her pencil on her visor. "Yep, that's about the going rate, so it's a deal. What's for dinner tonight, anyway? Give me something to look forward to."

"Barbeque plates from Bart's. He gives Kemp a good deal because he had three dogs and knows he'll need a payback some day."

"Smart guy. It never hurts to bank a few credits in the favor department." She stashed the writing implement and began to hunt for the business end of her paddle.

Delayne only hummed in response, too lost in her thoughts of how to get some credits in place with Kemp, too. Maybe her daddy could help her. Yes, the two men would get along swell, and she'd get the credit. Water trickled off the end of her paddle and soothed her disposition. When Eva thumped her paddle against the hull, she snapped out of her daydream in time to see a bittern lurking under a willow branch. She began to hum again, as if singing to the river for bringing her birds—without rock ledges standing in the way.

~

"You're too nice, Liv. I really shouldn't." Kemp shook his head, but the woman unloaded the white bags crimped full of popcorn anyway. Now, he had more than three barbeque boxes to balance, not that he was complaining.

"I've been meaning to get by, but haven't stepped one foot outside of my shop lately," she replied. The wind caught a wisp of her graying hair and she tucked it away to look up at him. "Becca called me Sunday afternoon. She had a visitor come by the doggie wash—the only pet groomer in Western Grove. When she heard Becca was coming over every Friday to Harrison, she wanted in on the action. They could ride together and split the cost of gas. What do you think, Doctor Junk?"

"I think I'm surrounded by a conspiracy of plotting women…and I love it." When he laughed, his load tried to shift. He tightened his grip around the boxes. "I had a follow-up ad in mind for the newspaper that could mention the groomer, if you give me her business name."

"Write it like a letter to the editor, thanking the good people of Harrison for their support of the rabies shot event. In closing, mention the groomer is coming with the doggie wash lady next week. That way, you've accomplished your mission of communicating the new service, and the paper gives it to you for free." She clapped her palms together like working magic.

"You are a gem, Liv. Every time I see you, it ends up saving me money." He leaned over to scrutinize her closer. "You're not my fairy godmother by any chance, are you?"

She pressed her hands to her chest. "Sakes, no. I hung up my wand years ago." The tiny wink she gave said otherwise.

"I'd better run. The pup's already in the car, and I need to deliver these Monday night specials while they're still hot."

"Give Delayne my best then. You owe me a visit next. I'll treat you to something new I've been mixing up."

"Count on it, maybe by Friday. We're off to see her father in Eustace Springs. I could bring him something tasty from your shop to make a solid first impression." He backed toward the car door.

"Like you need my help," she replied, getting the

door. The puppy gave a yelp from its crate and she baby-talked to it through the open window.

Kemp slid in and unloaded the dinner boxes into the passenger seat. The popcorn bags fell over but didn't leak any kernels, unfortunately. "Hey, what flavors did you send this time?"

She closed the door and stepped back from the curb. "Something dark and dessert-like. How's that for being mysterious?"

"Painfully good." He started the car and gave her a wave. Traffic seemed light and he got underway. In no time, the last building in town framed his side view mirror. The memory of his measly two-customer day faded. All he could think about was getting to Delayne and feeling alive again. Strappy yowled as though the countryside unleashed its wild side. It could have been the fresh air. *Fresh air and freedom from concern.* Or maybe it was the barbeque.

When he pulled up at Lost Creek, Delayne sat up on the stone wall out front waiting for him. He let the car roll to a stop and turned off the ignition. In seconds, he stood between her and the back door where the crate awaited. "Hey there, pretty lady. Which do you want first, your doggie or your dinner?"

She laughed and threw her arms open wide.

From her perch, she sat about eye level, a rare match-up. Kemp couldn't let it go without testing. He walked into her wingspan and soon soared from the connection. The puppy started to bark incessantly. "Okay, okay. I'm sure the feeling is mutual." He pulled away and got the crate out of the back seat.

"There's my big boy," she replied, clapping for possession.

Kemp eased the latch and held the door open to set the escapee loose. Strappy climbed right for Delayne's face and covered her with gracious licks of re-acquaintance. "Which renders me merely the delivery boy," he quipped, reaching through the window to get the dinner boxes. When he dangled the popcorn bags in front of Delayne, she squealed and tried to grab them. He held them too high for her to reach and arched his brows.

"Eva's in the kitchen," she said. "Go take those in and come back to get us, will you?"

"Won't I though? And you'd better be thinking about my tip for having to backtrack." He pushed though the door and turned to the kitchen, barely able to contain his elation.

Eva stood at the sink, smiling. "Thank goodness you're here. We're starved. That's what a good day on the river can do to you."

"Hey, Eva. How did Delayne do today?"

"She managed to stay off her leg…and consume a quarter of a pack of Oreos. I'd call that a good day."

"Then maybe all this dessert-flavored popcorn is wasted on you ladies."

"Oh, I wouldn't go that far, Doctor Junk. Man, that barbeque aroma is killing me."

"Let me get her inside then. Can you pour the tea?"

"Sure thing. And I'll take the puppy for a walk after dinner, so you two can be alone."

"Scrappy needs the exercise, so thanks." He shoved the screen door open with his palm and there sat Delayne, the puppy tucked into her neck, facing toward him. With the river bluffs as backdrop, the scene touched him to the core.

"See, baby? Daddy came back for you. Yes, he did."

Delayne's candy talk lured him to her, his heart cracking wide open. He rubbed his nose against the tip of hers and then lifted them both off the stone wall. She smelled like fresh rain, her hair still damp as it fell across his face. He'd have to tell her tonight, or explode with the revelation. When they approached the door, Eva held it open. He'd wait through dinner, and then all bets were off.

~

Delayne nibbled at the mocha popcorn Kemp had brought with dinner. The undercurrent of coffee flavor matched the wistful look in his eyes, sweet and full of longing. She took another bite as she cherished the thought of how they'd both arrived at the dock of affection's swift-flowing river at the same time. What a wonderment God had created with this emotion above all others. She could even forget about her knee soreness when swept up in its effect.

Eva passed by carrying the take-out containers to the trash can. At the last second, she read the recycling number on the bottom of the outer shell and rinsed them in the sink instead. The puppy's yip elongated into a yowl at being overlooked.

"No Strappy," Kemp said in a commanding tone. With a click of his fingers, the puppy reported to his side at the table.

"Looks like you two have come a long way." Delayne smiled and offered the popcorn in his direction.

Kemp took a few kernels and plunked them in his mouth with a nod.

"Lots of bonding going on this summer, if I'm not mistaken." She watched him long enough to see past his chewing pause. His amber eyes soon gave him away, a portal to a soul intent on her company. Would he be man enough to confess it—or bottle it up for safekeeping? That was the question, and today was as good a day as any to find out the answer. Restless, she stretched like a cat and felt his gaze fall on her again. *Mercy me.*

~

Tired of waiting for the perfect moment, Kemp decided to make one. When Eva mentioned walking out to get the mail after dinner, he handed her the dog's leash with a quick wink. Once he had trailed Delayne to the living room, he coaxed her outside to the patio.

She hobbled, the brace stiffening her gait. "Let's not go too far, as I'm running out of steps today."

"Meet me at the stone well over there." He made a broad gesture to usher her over.

She sighed and limped over the uneven stone pavers. "Thanks for dinner, by the way."

He smiled and leaned one hip against the rock work encasing the well. "You're most welcome. Anything to rebuild that knee of yours."

"If it didn't hurt to the touch, I'd let you massage it."

He held out a hand to draw her closer. "Maybe something more hands-off—like prayer—would be more appropriate for now."

"You brought me out here for prayer?" She gave him a protracted look.

Trapped in a corner, he thought to get at the heart of the matter—but not all at once. "I brought you out here for a special reason. Come sit with me."

Her questioning look dissolved in placation. She soon leaned beside him at the well.

"Let's get your weight off that leg." Kemp encircled her waist and lifted her high enough to sit on the edge of the stonework. Now things were getting cozy. "Do you know what I think about all day long?" He brushed her cheek with his index finger.

"Erosion banks like me? I'm seeing them in my sleep." She rolled her eyes and arched back, stretching.

He enjoyed the playful exchange, as she was see-through honest about her time-consuming assignment. "No, not hardly. I think about…you. My focus dissolves and the next thing I know, you come strolling right into my thoughts."

A smile twitched at her lips. "Hmm. I'd diagnose that as a bad case of attentiveness, Doctor Junkowski." She blinked and took her time opening her eyes again. Her stare intensified, her eyes a soft velvety green in the evening light.

"I believe I'm falling under a curious spell, little bird." He shifted closer and took her hand in his. "It's light like a floating bubble or a drifting cloud. When it has me in its grip, there's not a worry in the sky—only loveliness—and my appreciation of it."

She tipped her chin up. "Sounds atmospheric."

"Oh, it's a magnetic anomaly, all right. A rare phenomenon." His words practically tumbled onto her cheek, he stood so close.

"Does your sky loveliness have a name?" she asked in a whisper.

He drew his bottom lip along the arch of her brow. A hush fell over the patio and even the crickets ceased their chirping. "It must be love," he replied soft and low, for her ears only. With a tilt of his head, he slipped closer yet and gave her a kiss to set the cloud adrift again.

Beyond cooperative, Delayne gave a throaty moan as the embrace lifted weightless through time. Soon, a barking puppy crashed the private moment. Strappy ran up and attempted to scramble into her lap.

Eva stepped up from the side yard, her eyes open so wide that her bangs hid her arched eyebrows. "Sorry for the intrusion, guys, but I think someone's been tampering with the garage. It seems odd. I never noticed the scuff marks before tonight."

Delayne's forehead wrinkled, her gaze wandering down the water trough toward the outbuildings. "Kemp, I need to check this out—but I'm exhausted and can hardly afford one more step."

Their privacy shattered, he hated to separate, so he scooped her up in his arms instead. He stepped up into the bowl of the water trough and followed its path down the slope to check out the matter. The puppy yipped the whole way down, trying to get at his feet.

Delayne's finger stroked his beard as she gazed at him intently. The look in her eyes spoke of something more to be said, despite the interruption.

Having jogged ahead, Eva soon held the unfastened hasp in her hand.

Kemp lowered Delayne to the ground and held her a few seconds longer than necessary.

She pointed to the left of the door. "Look. Scrape marks in the rocks. I think Eva might be right."

"There's only one way to find out what's making them," he replied. Laying a shoulder into the door, he tugged it open. In the gleam of dusk, the building's contents became apparent—row upon row of car bumpers.

Eva's brow arched like a cat's back. "Well, I'll be a monkey's uncle."

Kemp ran a rough count and had upwards of three dozen in a matter of seconds. A trembling hand soon crept across his arm.

"The motor pool thefts," Delayne whispered, "all collecting right here under my nose."

"Plus more," Kemp added. The hair on the back of his neck began to stand on end. The object of his newfound affection lived way too close to the contraband for his comfort. His next breath seemed to pinch. "Looks like someone's running a lucrative chop shop."

"Good God above, that's grand theft auto," Eva replied, paling under her freckles.

Delayne's bottom lip trembled as she stood staring, her mouth agape.

Knowing he had to maneuver past the disarming discovery, he thought about park headquarters and began to formulate a plan. "We've got to show this to Manning tomorrow morning." Repulsed at the subversive nature of the crime, Kemp had the sudden urge to spit, but couldn't make it happen to save his life. "Someone obviously forgot to reset the lock."

"A numbskull move at that," Eva replied.

"And one we won't repeat," Delayne added. "I'm setting the front door lock as soon as Kemp leaves for town."

Though off balance from the disclosure of the garage contents, Kemp had no intention of allowing the evening to draw to a close like the bang from a cap gun. He glanced over at Delayne and her gaze locked with his. "Come down to the river with me before I go." He looked deeper into her eyes and hoped she wouldn't object.

She lifted her arms toward him instead, which was all the invitation he needed.

~

The river seemed to acquire the luminescence of the low hanging moon as its waters ran past the stone steps at Lost Creek. Delayne nestled back against Kemp's chest and took comfort in the rhythm of his respirations. She held at bay all the phantoms that called for her attention, which included unfinished canoe trips, a ruffed grouse project that needed a finalized map, and untested fingerprints on a series of chrome bumpers in her garage. Instead, a man with honorable intentions now held her at the water's edge.

"You're quiet." He curled around one shoulder and planted his cheek near hers.

"Just enjoying the company. Plus, the river seems to have absorbed the moonlight."

"So magical." He wrapped both arms around her and gave her waist a squeeze.

She leaned back onto him and became less precarious on the stone step in his grip. "You make the ledge of love quite the lofty place for a girl to visit, you know that?"

He swiped his whiskers across her cheek. "I hope that means it's a place you want to go."

"I definitely do, Kemp. I'm falling for you. And I see it in your eyes, too."

"Then love me with an open heart—and I'll do the

same." With his pledge came the seal, and his kiss lasted until the moon withdrew its shimmer from the river.

She nuzzled into his neck to extend their last moments together. "Will you let me have the puppy back tonight? We'll see each other in the morning when you come to headquarters. You can have Strappy then."

"Okay, though it makes me the odd man out."

"But he's my guard dog."

"Good point. You win."

"Thank you. Now carry me back to the ranch house, will you?"

"I don't want to—but I will." He shifted away from her to stand and soon tapped her shoulder.

Delayne struggled to her feet, tired from the day and cramped from her chronic position in the canoe. Tomorrow would be another day of the same, after making an appearance at the office. Eva had passed Lost Creek on her survey route so they'd put in further down the river, which was north on the map, a crazy juxtaposition. Suddenly, Kemp swirled her up into his arms and the whole night turned cartwheels. She lost her bearings just like that and fell back onto his chest. Maybe she could trust him to realign with the planets on the way up to the house. What a reliance on dependable orientation. She had Kemp and he had her. *Remarkable.*

Chapter 12

A downpour cloaked the entrance to the headquarters parking lot. Delayne missed the first turn-in and strained to catch her last option. She'd left Eva sleeping late at Lost Creek, the rain tossing a wet blanket on their canoe float to complete the upper river. When the curb dipped below the rapid run-off, she veered left and let the car creep by the motor pool fleet.

An hour early for the regular workday to begin, it surprised her to see two vehicles already claiming the closest spaces in the employee parking area. She eyed her rain slicker and opted to pull into a spot well away from the jacked-up truck. Cutting a praise song off the radio, she pocketed the keys and tugged the slicker into service.

With Kemp dropping by at eight-thirty to help deliver the garage news to Manning, she had the better part of an hour to start finalizing the ruffed grouse survey map. At the end of the month, her career would tumble into the abyss of unemployment. The postcard in her purse from the University of Arizona could possibly bridge that span, but chasing sage grouse through their arid habitat seemed less than scintillating as an option. She stepped into the downpour and her hood crumpled against her face.

Her foot landed in sheeting water flow with the first step. The brace clamping her injured knee would soon be drenched. She hastened into a limping run which splattered her pants. A drying out period would be in order. Hopefully, hot coffee could be an integral part of that.

The rear office door opened when she tugged at it. Though the lights weren't on in the hall, a light illuminated the interior offices. Deciding against leaving a trail of water through the building, she shirked out of the slicker and hooked it on a rack outside the employee break room.

As she headed for her office area, muted voices echoed from the open lab area where her map work awaited. Intrigued, Delayne tossed her pack into her chair and headed in that general direction. A male voice amplified with a swear word. She smoothed her hair back and made the instantaneous decision to make an appearance despite the volatile exchange.

"You get some kind of lock out there ASAP," the same voice insisted.

She hesitated at the mention of a lock. Kemp had noted the absence of one out at Lost Creek. Though compelled to see who was having the conversation, an undercurrent of threat made her next step a tough one. Dread pinched her chest as she paused in the unlit room, recognizing a threshold where angels feared to tread. For an instant, she questioned the crossing.

A response came from the second person in the conversation that sounded like an affirmation from a wounded animal, low and throaty. In seconds, footsteps faded toward the back exit and the door banged closed. Another reactive explicative echoed off the walls.

She stepped toward the door, but the sole of her boot separated and dug into the carpet. As she wrestled to free it by flexing her sore leg, the light extinguished in the lab. Panicked, she pivoted toward the outer wall and held her breath. The entangled boot broke free to aid her maneuver right before the lab occupant exited. Separated a mere arm's length, she strained to identify the staffer, but couldn't make out his silhouette.

An eternity of seconds passed as the footsteps dissipated in the direction of the senior staff office wing. Paralysis made her frame ache, tacked against the wall. Kemp filtered into her thoughts like a lifeline of stability. Instantly, the urge to flee the building struck. She could wait for him in her car. There, they could disclose this whole ugly thing to Manning in seclusion and shift the burden to his broad shoulders.

In a few quaking steps, she retraced her route to her office cubicle. Before retrieving her pack, she shucked a thick rubber band from the base of her pencil holder and snapped it around the toe of the boot, drawing the separated sole back together. With a death grip on the pack, she turned toward the rear exit and breathed a prayer for protection. Thunder rumbled and brought the slicker to mind.

Her steps fell even across the distance, with her weight shifted to her toes to keep the boots from squishing. The black space she had forded with enthusiasm less than five minutes ago now seemed inhospitable. Recalling the infamous "seven minutes of hell" experienced by the Mars rover staff prior to its successful tumble-down landing, she squared her shoulders with newfound resolve. She would escape and expose this wormwood in the department. She had to.

Above the corridor, the faint light of a smoke detector cast a pallid illumination up ahead, which became her next destination. From that point, all she had to do was bank right, grab the slicker, and bound out of the exit. She kept up the rhythm of her pace and claimed protection on loan from the Almighty.

A metallic clank rippled from the office hall, now just off her left shoulder. She quickened her pace, passed the tiny spot of illumination, and held her breath. Suddenly, a shock of bluish-white light filtered into the hall through a glass-paneled door. Braving a glance in the direction, she pinpointed the occupied office.

In seconds, the slicker fell within reach. She tossed the hood over her head and stepped out into the drenching rain. The distance closed to her car. As she passed the first parking space, only a slurry of mud remained where the jacked-up truck had been.

She clicked the fob to unlock the car door. The taillights flashed like rescue beacons. She eased the door open and slid inside, the pack tucked to her ribs. A flash of lightning tore across the distance. Lucid in the moment, she counted the doors down the hall from memory, assigning senior staff members to each room as she went.

She squeezed her eyes closed when the occupant of

the fourth office claimed unmistakable involvement. "Good God above, help me," she prayed through numb lips. Given her best estimation, Ross Connors was part of the chop shop thefts plaguing the department.

A pang from her knee reminded her to elevate her leg. She propped her foot atop the brake pedal. Sordid thoughts raced to the surface. Had Ross been intentionally routing her away from something by taking her into marginal habitat upslope? Chills ran down her back. She planted her face in her hands and wiped the wetness away.

Time went liquid as she visualized her route map and began redirecting transects in a down slope layout. Toward the bottom of the old logging road lay the mountain berg of Ponca. A spotted dog came to mind next, and it didn't take much of a logical wander to wind up at Tommy Lee Resnick's spread down the highway. She reached up and locked the door.

Apprehension needled deeper when she considered the possibility that Connors might be in cahoots with Tommy Lee. That certainly explained why Manning's efforts to tighten motor pool protocol had failed to stop the rash of recent thefts. When she recalled how Connors was quick to side with Tommy Lee at the burn boss training episode, her chest tightened. Together, they represented a formidable foe, a lethal combo of executive access and prodigal pilfering.

Delayne shut her eyes and attempted to regain her rational calm. She leaned against the door, her temple soon touching cool glass. Out of nowhere, a knuckle knock exploded on the window, falling like a mortar strike in the downpour. She did what any red-blooded female would do and screamed to highest heaven.

~

"Blame me." Kemp stroked the top of Delayne's hand with his thumb. Water dripped off his hood, but he focused on the frightened woman in his grip. "I thought you were signaling me over with your flashing brake lights. I didn't mean to startle you out of your skin."

She stared out over the steering wheel. "We have trouble. Compound trouble."

He hooked her chin with a finger and turned her face toward him. "Do you mean beyond a garage full of stolen bumpers?"

She nodded, her eyes widening. "I came in early to finish my map and almost walked into a secret debriefing. You might be interested to know that the crux of the exchange concerned a missing lock. One guy swore at the disclosure, and the other departed posthaste after being ordered to get a replacement."

He shook his head in appeasement. "Well, well. So the pot begins to boil."

"Given the weather, it's more like overflowing. One of my boots fell apart from all the puddles." She shrugged her shoulders. "Maybe I should call and wake up Eva to put her on watch for a visitor out back."

"I was thinking we should go straight out there ourselves…with Manning, of course. I'll let him call that shot. Who was the remaining staffer? Could you tell?"

She dropped her forehead until it pressed the steering wheel. "I didn't see anyone, but a light came on down the senior office hall, the fourth door on the left."

"Do you know whose office that is?"

A dread-filled moan escaped her throat. "Ross

Connors. That's what has me so spooked, I guess."

A pair of headlights swept across the parking lot, piercing the rain. In seconds, a large SUV swept by. "Hey, that looks like Manning's Yukon."

"Yes, it's probably him, right on time."

"Hold tight. I'll go intercept him and bring him in here for collaboration on what to do next. You might clear a spot on the back seat for him. Hey, where's the puppy?"

"Strappy's home sleeping the day away with Eva. Wish I could say the same."

"Be right back." Sliding from the car, Kemp huddled under his rain jacket and began to sprint toward the director's reserved parking spot. The man soon emerged balancing a travel cup despite the downpour. "Mr. Manning—something's up regarding the motor pool thefts. Delayne's waiting in her car so we can maintain privacy, if you don't mind."

His eyebrows shot up under the brim of his rain hat. After a second's hesitation, he turned back to the parking lot. "Crazy weather. The river's liable to be up after this. I'm glad Delayne isn't out there under these conditions. We'll let the erosion win out today."

"Yes, sir. I agree. Unfortunately, the forecast makes the rest of the week look soggy."

"Oh, great."

Kemp opened the rear door and gestured inside. Delayne's face appeared over the console. She attempted a brittle smile. He ducked into the front seat and lowered his hood. "Thank you for your discretion, sir. I'll start since Delayne has been shaken up this morning."

Manning unzipped his raincoat and gave her a

searching glance.

When Delayne leaned back in the driver's seat with a sigh, Kemp continued. "Last night at Lost Creek, Eva discovered something odd about the garage while out walking the dog. It was unlocked. Since that seemed out of the ordinary, we all went to investigate. When we opened the door, we were stunned to see rows and rows of car bumpers, like a horde of detached chrome waiting to be exported."

Manning inhaled sharply. "You're saying that door is typically locked solid?"

Delayne turned, her eyes hollow with fear. "Yes, sir. In fact, I've never seen it unlocked before. I always assumed the department used it for storage of some kind."

"Of course, your motor pool thefts came to mind, though we weren't exactly sure what elements had gone missing. At that point, it wasn't too farfetched to speculate it could have been bumpers." Kemp wiped at a drip from his cuff.

"Among other items, which I'm not at liberty to disclose," Manning replied.

"We only wanted to report what we found last night, but Delayne ran into something more this morning. It seemed to be connected, so that's why I waylaid you for our satellite meeting here."

Manning threw his palm up. "I want to hear this part first person. Ms. Davidson, give me your direct account."

She swallowed and her lips parted for a few silent seconds. "I came in early to get some mapping work done prior to our scheduled meeting. Two vehicles were already in the lot, but I didn't think anything of it.

Even though the office was unlocked, it was dark inside—all but the rear lab where my master map was waiting. I stopped by my cubicle where I overheard some kind of heated exchange between two men back in the lab. One man swore at the mention of a missing lock, and then demanded the other party get a replacement as soon as possible. The second guy stormed out and the lab went dark, so I froze in place. Deciding my car was the safest place to retreat, I hobbled back out into the storm."

"Good move, all things considered," Manning replied. "You didn't get a look at either man?"

Delayne's mouth fell open, but no words escaped.

"Sir, as I understand it, a light came on down the senior office hall," Kemp added. He slid a hand beyond the console to touch Delayne's slicker. Her pinkie finger soon clasped his.

"Tell me, Ms. Davidson. I assure you, I'll hold it in the strictest confidence. Whose office illuminated as you left?" Manning leaned forward and placed an open hand across the console as though to validate his claim.

Delayne turned to him, paler than a ghost. "Ross Connors, sir. Fourth door on the left. Count it for yourself."

Kemp sat in silent tension as the car windows began to fog over. What would happen next said everything about Manning's willingness to address the whole convoluted matter. Delayne had done her part, which he'd be sure to express to her later. He strummed his thumb across her knuckles and waited.

"Were the two vehicles still in the lot when you returned to your car?"

"No, sir. The jacked-up truck had left mud in its

space, but was nowhere to be seen."

"We'll check the employee vehicle registry, but half our staff members drive a truck. Still, we have an advantage to play."

Kemp turned to the back seat. "How so, Dave?"

"The hardware store doesn't open for another hour and a half. Let's go to Lost Creek and take a look at some contraband chrome. Or would you prefer that I drive, Delayne?"

Kemp shifted his glance with a wink.

She cleared her throat. "No, sir. I've got this. Driving will give me something positive to focus on."

"Good. I hope it doesn't bother your bad knee."

"What bad knee, sir?" She keyed the ignition and checked her mirrors.

Kemp eased his expression to one laced with admiration and caught her gaze when she turned to back out. Their advantage rode on a solitary free-standing hasp, one he'd take, given the shut-tight case. When his thoughts shifted to Lost Creek, he recognized another missing element he could rectify. "I'm getting my dog back when we get to your stone ranch. A veterinarian can't be without his canine companion."

"*Your* dog?" Delayne questioned, fighting to prevent a subtle smile.

The seatbelt warning chimed and he reached for his restraint in a dodge of latent guilt.

"You know," Manning said, "this might explain some of the tension building between you and Connors."

Delayne pulled out onto the main road through Harrison and headed for Lost Creek. "You're referring to his tendency to route me away from the obvious, so

I'm risking my neck on those upper ledges?" The car lurched forward in response to her uneven acceleration.

"Hmmm. Did I miss the obvious?" Manning's seatbelt clicked into place.

Kemp chewed his lip, wondering if he'd missed it also.

"I mentally plotted the survey routes in the opposite direction—one that contains suitable habitat. It drops me right into Ponca by the upper falls."

"What's up there that could be suspicious? We have several derelict houses taken under eminent domain in Ponca. That hillbilly hideout is as innocuous as they come."

Something relevant came to mind and Kemp sensed that alluding to it would be, by far, the best exposure. "Dave, just because we're dealing with the backyard of Dogpatch, USA, that doesn't mean Daisy Mae might not have something to hide. Remember, I lost my spare tire in Ponca." The car tires threw grit in a slip of traction as the vehicle made its way up a rising grade to chase the headwaters of the iconic river that scratched the bedrock with aqua blue.

~

With three weeks left in her tenure as an expert researcher, Delayne sensed her credibility wobble as though stretched in a sling. They waited for Eva on the rear stone patio as the rain began to let up. Kemp made small talk regarding his clinic, prompting Manning to offer rookie suggestions for boosting his business. Finally, the back door opened and Eva came out clad in a cheap plastic poncho. From its wrinkles, it seemed to be on debut duty.

"Okay. I think we're all set," Delayne said.

Eva poked the camera out underneath her rainproof sheath.

"I have my cell phone camera also," Manning said. "I can send photos of evidence right to the federal investigator's office."

"That definitely one-ups me," Eva replied. "My shots will be backup, so let me know what more you need."

Delayne led the way, following the winding stone trough.

"I always thought this watering system was pure genius," Manning mumbled.

Kemp came up by his side. "My sentiments exactly. Let's hope there's a turn of clever still waiting to be claimed out here."

Delayne held her palm out, and it remained dry for the first time all morning. To celebrate, she lowered her hood and shook her hair loose. "Here's one musty garage, now coming up on the left." As she approached, her tension ebbed. The door remained unlocked.

"Here, wait," Manning insisted. "Eva, take a shot of the hasp there before we open up." He stepped into the lead and produced his phone.

Delayne glanced at Kemp hopeful for moral support, but he seemed preoccupied with a rivulet of mud cutting through the driveway gravel. Steaming under her slicker, she unfastened the closures and let the gentle breeze off the river begin to cool her.

Manning stooped and shot an exposure of something in the mud. "Paint chips, like something rubbed against the door. It might mean something."

"Well, well. Look at this," Kemp insisted. He dug a finger into the gravel and soon a weathered lock dangled from it, caked in mud.

"I'll take the not-so-missing lock," Manning replied. "It looks like standard park issue." When Eva offered him a plastic zip bag, he took it with a nod. Pocketing the evidence, he locked gazes with Delayne. "It's now or never. Let's open up and have a look-see."

She blinked to clear her vision and soon felt a reassuring hand on the small of her back. Kemp stepped to her side and placed his other hand on the upper edge of the door. With determination, she threw the hasp clear and yanked the door open. Even with the rain-darkened morning, it soon became clear that nothing had changed. Uncountable rows of chrome and black bumpers smiled back at them from the garage's interior. Relief washed away her last worry.

Manning stepped inside, his chest heaving with deep breaths. "Let me get pictures, and then I want a count. Doc, you take the chrome and Delayne, you count the black ones. We'll try to stay out in case they've left some footprints or something the investigator can use."

"Got it, chief," Kemp replied. Eva handed him a flashlight. He dipped in front of Delayne to direct its beam. When it gleamed on shiny metal, he turned and gave her an impish grin. "He assigned me the pretty chrome ones." Dark brows waggled above his honey-hued eyes.

"Favorite child," she snipped in response. She dodged around his restraining arm and got superior position for making the count. This was her backyard, after all.

Chapter13

Kemp followed the road signs to Eustace Springs, glad to leave the main highway behind.

"Any trepidation before meeting Daddy?" Delayne asked from the passenger seat.

"Not on my part. Remember, I'm the one who suggested the jaunt. Getting away has a certain beckon to it—and besides, he's my mentor. I need to get his input on the groomer deal."

"Right. The groomer deal." Dimples soon dotted her cheeks.

"What? You think this is some sort of check-me-out, don't you? Like he's going to evaluate me to see if I'm good enough to date his daughter, is that it?"

"All I can say is stand up straight, answer his questions in complete sentences, and try to come off as college-educated. That should make for a strong start." She returned her focus to the crossword puzzle book in her lap.

He regarded the pink-blooming crabapples in the roadside landscaping as they merged onto a tree-lined street. "I speaks real good, no worries." He leaned toward her and flicked her pencil point. "Plus, I'm ten times better than the last guy you brought home."

She cleared her throat and shoved the pencil's eraser across the marked page. "That's easy, since there was no last guy. You get full scrutiny from a highly evaluative man, so congratulations."

"Okay. A tiny sliver of trepidation now enters the scene. But we're both veterinarians. Plus, we've already hit it off over the phone." He flexed his hands off the steering wheel as though to ward off any misgivings.

She pointed ahead. "Turn right at the stop sign. That will put us four miles short of a dead reckoning between mentor and wannabe."

He protested with a low growl. "Make that welcome wannabe." The car halted for the sign, but no traffic appeared in either direction. They must still be well outside of town yet.

"Yes, you're right, a welcome wannabe." A smile flitted up with her retraction.

"Are we early? Gaylord isn't on lunch break yet, is he?"

"We're plenty early. It's only eleven forty-five. Besides, it's not a lunch break. The animal clinic closes at noon on Saturdays. Daddy wants to take you fishing out back on his secret creek. Tell me that's not special treatment."

"Maybe, but not the special treatment I had in mind at the moment."

When she looked up and discovered no traffic in sight, she leaned toward him. "I don't believe I've ever had the pleasure of kissing you during the morning hours, Doctor Junkowski. Would that be forward of me?"

"Probably, but you only have fifteen minutes to venture an attempt." He shifted the car out of gear and released her seatbelt. An unmistakable magnetism drew him to her.

"I'm kind of hoping Daddy likes you a little," she admitted, climbing past the middle console. Her fingertips found his beard line and the puppy yipped from the back seat.

"And why's that, Ms. Davidson?" he whispered as she drew near. "Could it be that you more than like me a little?"

"Let me remind myself." Her lips landed in a sumptuous spot right on his as she took full advantage of the unplanned stop.

Straining against his seat belt, Kemp leaned toward her as far as possible to make the moment last. The sweet scent of fruit trees in bloom filled the country lane. A violin solo played on the radio and deepened the spell. When she eventually pulled away, he held her arm. "Love me as much as I love you." The begging tone that accompanied the request had been unintentional.

"I dearly hope and pray that's for you to discover." She looked up at him through her lashes as a blush reddened her neck.

He stroked the reaction with his thumb, reluctant to let her go. Her skin felt infinitely soft, fueling his attraction. "I suppose fishing with Daddy is the next logical step, then." He quirked a one-sided smile as she slid back into her seat. "Was it a right turn you requested?"

"Yes, a right turn. Oh, look at the time. If you hurry, I can help Daddy close up." She snapped her seat belt in place to accentuate the claim.

"One on-time arrival, coming right up." He swerved onto the secondary road and let the forward momentum take the place of her magnetic draw, a cheap replacement—even if physics dictated it for a body in motion.

~

Delayne rushed inside to surprise her father as his voice echoed from the back exam room. A gray-haired woman stepped out, her vacant eyes rimmed with red. The snap of a cotton sheet brought her attention to the matter at hand—the loss of a beloved pet. She continued toward the back room to see if she could offer any assistance. Kemp started through the door, held it for the grief-stricken client, and followed her back outside.

"Hey, Daddy. Sorry to walk in on such a somber note." She leaned toward him and gave him a kiss on the cheek. His skin felt clammy, especially for having the AC running.

"Glad you've come, Delayne. It'll help cheer things up around here. This Welch corgi had been a patient for fourteen years. That's a pretty good run in dog years. Of course, Alice wants me to put him out by the creek, so my work's not done for the day—yet."

"I brought some brute strength with me—the tall, dark, and handsome kind. I bet we can solicit his help to get the deed done." She picked the corner of the sheet up and took a look at the faithful canine.

He harrumphed and recorded the death in the

animal's file.

"Get what deed done?" Kemp asked, stepping into the doorway.

"We need a final resting spot for this corgi," she replied. "Daddy, I'd like you to meet Kemp Junkowski."

Her father rose slowly, regarding the visitor's considerable height. "I'm Gaylord Davidson. It's nice to meet you at long last." He extended his hand and Kemp shook it.

"We tried to get here earlier, but there was a busted knee, a teething puppy, and a whole lot of rain in the way, sir."

He brushed his hand through the air as though to sweep them out. "Extenuating circumstances seem to evaporate when the time is truly right. You couldn't have picked a better weekend, really."

"That's great to hear, Daddy. I can't wait for you to meet Strappy. Kemp has him trained to obey a whistle command, and I taught him to sit. Hope you don't mind seeing spots for awhile. I'll bring him in once we get Kemp on task for the burial."

"I'd be happy to, sir. Just tell me where the shovel is…and where you want the grave." He stepped back outside the small room as though to signal his readiness.

Gaylord wiped his face and adjusted his glasses back square on the bridge of his nose. "Why am I so wiped out this morning? DeeDee, honey. You pick the burial site. Anywhere left of the footbridge on this side of the creek bank is fine. Take old Henry out with you as you go. I'll close up shop posthaste and get ready to do something more fun with my company."

Delayne placed her hand on his arm. "That's a deal. Do you still have the caddy or should we just use the sheet?"

He gestured to the far corner of the building. "The same utility closet holds the shovel and the caddy. I'll let you reacquaint yourself while I head for the gentlemen's room."

Kemp nodded and headed for the front door.

Delayne crossed the threshold right behind him and noticed how faded the clinic sign had become. "Hey, maybe I can spruce up Daddy's sign while we're here." She led the way to the storage room and broke a few spider webs opening its door.

"I had the opportunity to speak a few words of comfort to Miss Alice as I walked her to her car. They emphasized positive closure in vet school, but I haven't had much of a chance to apply my training in that area."

"I'm sure Daddy will appreciate hearing that. Now let's get that corgi laid to rest. Leave the shovel here against the building while we bring it out here. Then I'll show you the creek and we'll pick a shady spot."

"No tree roots," he added with certainty.

"No, just sandy soil with an occasional rock. But nothing like we have along the Buffalo." She drew out the canvas gurney and eyed the tattered seam along one carrying pole. "I think this will hold."

Kemp brought out the shovel and followed her back inside. When they slid the old canine off the table, he took the lead. In short order, they were back along the winding creek under a fringing canopy of red maples. "How about along here? This looks restful."

She lowered her end to the ground and dusted off her hands. "Perfect. Can I leave you with this? I hardly got to speak to Daddy at all. I'll wipe down the exam tables and help him lock up. Plus, I need to set Strappy free on the front lawn."

"Sure, I've got this. Want me to come around to the house side once I finish?"

"Yes, use the front door. You know, like a real guest." She scrunched up her nose so he'd know she was teasing and got waved off with the shovel blade. Excited to show off her pet, she backtracked to the car and removed the carrier. Upon release, the pup christened the grass and found an interesting tree. "Come on, baby. Let's go meet Grandpa Gaylord. He has some doggie treats inside." She hoisted the dog, set on making the encounter happen.

Delayne pushed through the door and found her father sitting behind the front counter, right where she'd seen him a thousand times before. She placed the wiggly Dalmatian on the counter and let go. "Ta-da. Here's Strappy."

Her father looked up, but instead of reaching for the dog, he clutched his chest. A gurgling gasp deepened into a groan as he attempted to stand. Fear iced his gaze. His legs buckled and he collapsed on the front counter beside the wiggly pup. Unable to hold him, the counter became a stepping-stone to the floor, where he crumbled and lay stock-still.

Numb with astonishment, Delayne skirted the edge of the front desk and knelt beside him. She dug the base of his neck for a pulse and found a weak one. "Oh, Daddy. No…" The quiver in her voice tried to send the quake to her knees, but she stood and shot a glance at the door. That's when the glass-fronted cabinet sporting a red cross came to her attention. "An AED. Thank you,

Lord above."

A surreal calm came over her as she crossed to open the cabinet. She knew a squawked warning would ensue, but she was ready. Its immediate protest fell like music to her ears because it announced that the battery would be strong enough for the discharge. *Good.* She had a hurried suspicion she would need the whole works.

Only when she returned and rolled her father on his back did it occur to her that Kemp was close enough to help. She'd take him up on that in a heartbeat, but first, she'd honor him by following the training he'd insisted on the day they officially met. After clearing the shirt buttons, she reached for the razor and pressed the AED start switch. Seconds flew by but she knew not to waste them. The puppy yowled from its perch on the counter. She shushed it like a restless baby.

Soon the paddles were in hand and the prep work over. "Come on, come on, machine. Hang in there, Daddy. Please, Lord, let him hang in there." With the paddles affixed, she crept back and allowed the device to go about redeeming its reputation as a lifesaver. The voltage amped up and, this time, the procedure ran its full circuit. His flaccid body jumped with the electric discharge and she waited with breath held for the results.

Suddenly, Kemp bent over the counter, grabbing the pup out of the way. "Have you called nine-one-one yet?"

"No, no time for that," she replied without looking at him.

Buttons pressed on the landline phone. "We have a medical emergency… ambulance, please." He tapped her foot with his. "Take the pulse again." He shifted the desk chair out of the way. "Yes, the AED fully deployed."

"We have a pulse," Delayne said. She turned to him and a sob wracked her shoulders.

"We have a pulse. Yes, we'll be ready." Kemp lowered the phone and put the puppy back on the counter. His hand slid from the top of her head to her shoulder. Stooping, he collected her against his side. "Great job, Layne. You've kept him alive. The ambulance is on the way."

A lump choked her throat closed as she watched a shallow respiration fill her father's chest. The whole scene began to blur as tears welled up in her eyes.

A metallic click sounded from the device. "Patient stabilizing," it declared in automated certainty. "Detach apparatus while awaiting transport."

She reached for the closest paddle and discovered Kemp's steady hand right there with hers. She yielded to his expertise and snuggled to his side, so close his every movement seemed to be her own. That lent comfort beyond understanding. Before she knew it, the EMTs were alongside to hasten the rescue. The puppy yipped and wagged its tail, hopeful for more attention. She lifted Strappy and pressed the puppy to her chest, hopeful to quell the heartache inside.

Kemp nodded to the lead medic and came back toward her. "You ride with them. I'll close up and be right behind you once I get Strappy situated." He stole the dog and bent to give her a peck on the cheek, his amber eyes holding all the warmth of a summer day.

"Thanks for freeing me up to stay with Daddy. Use the kennel run behind the house."

She stepped into the side door of the ambulance and took one last look at him. The heart-tug was unmistakable. The attendant slammed the door, trapping her inside. She mouthed "I love you" through the window and pointed at her heart.

Kemp tucked the puppy under his chin and blinked his farewell message.

Delayne let the ambulance's forward momentum plant her squarely in the seat. She automatically reached for the seatbelt restraint, her numbed thoughts limping in a thousand directions. The steady blip of the heart monitor cut through the haze and sounded more like the abiding presence of God to her. Deep-down thankful, she remembered to pray for her father's recovery the remainder of the way to the hospital.

~

On the verge of leaving, Kemp dug the keys from his pocket as a SUV pulled into the clinic's lot. The prominent muzzle of a greyhound soon appeared out of the rear window. Interested, he approached the driver's side. "Sorry ma'am. The clinic's closed."

A middle-aged woman lowered the glass. "Oh, that's okay. Gaylord said to come after hours and he'd clean Rebel's teeth for me."

He opened his stance as if standing over a threshold, Sure, he could explain the situation and refuse service, but it went against everything he'd been attempting to establish the last four months. Though it wasn't his clinic, he could most certainly do the work. "Allow me to introduce myself. I'm Kemp Junkowski, DVM. Doctor Gaylord has been mentoring me as of late. He's not able to do the work right now, but I would be happy to. It's up to you, ma'am."

"Gosh, I'm already two months late getting the cleaning done, not to mention that I live almost twenty miles out. Yes, let's get this taken care of today, if you're not in a hurry." She nodded at his keys by way of explanation.

He pocketed the keys with a smile. "No hurry at all. Let me walk back through the house and unlock the clinic door. You might give Rebel a chance to mark the front lawn while I'm doing that, for best results."

She laughed and eased the car up to a parking header. "One dual purpose walk, coming right up."

He tossed her a good-natured wave and quelled the excitement of transitioning back to a vet out of the blue. A glance at his watch reminded him he had plenty of time, as getting Gaylord admitted to cardiac ICU would take hours. He'd call Delayne afterwards to explain his delay. Soon, he found himself standing at the clinic's door welcoming a muscle-bound canine client with energy to spare. What a beast.

"Just to warn you, he's not fond of this teeth cleaning business," the owner said.

"Well, let's see if I can charm him into cooperating then." Kemp rubbed two fingers up the dog's snout and quickly found a sweet spot between its ears. "Lead Rebel into the first room there and we'll get down to business."

"But Gaylord uses the middle room for dental work."

"Fine then. That's where the equipment will be. Thank you for pointing that out." He gestured to the second alcove and followed her in for a tussle of race hound proportion, a challenge he welcomed, even on a Saturday.

~

Delayne couldn't put a finger on the source of her mounting annoyance until she checked the time on her phone. No messages waited. It had been over an hour. Could Kemp have gotten lost on the way to the hospital? All kinds of scenarios started coming to mind when the swish of a white lab coat distracted her.

A small-framed doctor checked his clipboard and looked back at her. "Are you here for Gaylord Davidson, ma'am?"

"Yes, I'm his daughter." Her annoyance drained into something more intense.

"Fine. We have him headed to his room in ICU. I took a look at the EKG and the blockage shown is very minor. My best strategy is to insert a stent, place him on a restricted diet, and call it sufficient. It could have been a lot worse. I understand he has you to thank for such a speedy resuscitation. That will work to his advantage."

"Thank you, doctor. When do you think the stent can be inserted?"

"I scheduled it for five-fifteen this evening, if that works for your family."

"Yes—and it's only me here with Daddy. I filled out the admissions form."

"Then we're all set. I'd suggest moving to the ICU waiting room on the second floor."

"Can I see him before the surgery?" She stood to reinforce her position.

"He's sedated right now, but I'll let the nursing staff know you'd like to be notified when he wakes up. I'm sure there are a few things you'd like to say, Miss Davidson." He stepped back toward the ER.

"Thank you, doctor. See you on the second floor

then." Delayne sat down and whipped out her phone. In seconds, she had the crux of the message typed into a text and sent to Kemp. At least he'd have the latest update, wherever he was.

~

At three o'clock, Kemp had filed Rebel's paperwork, washed up, and made plans to walk right out the clinic door, locking it behind him. He stood and tidied up the phone cord. The door hinges squeaked and a man wearing a plaid shirt appeared with a large box. Toenails scraped at the cardboard inside. Intrigued, he stood and walked toward him. "What can I do for you this afternoon?"

The man looked around with skittering eyes. "Uh, Doc said to come late and he'd get this litter cleaned up for me to sell. They're pureblooded and due to go on the market in two weeks."

"I'm Doctor Kemp Junkowski, filling in for Doctor Davidson. He's had a medical emergency and is still at the hospital. I'd be happy to administer the treatment if you know what you want."

"Yep. Shots, de-worming, and their tails bobbed. I've got to get it done before they get any bigger." His chewed his gum and waited for an answer.

Kemp considered the commitment. He could repeat the routine no more than four times to be done in a reasonable amount of time. One glimpse into the box told him he'd be maxed out. Four wavy-coated spaniel puppies looked back at him. "Are you planning to pay in cash?"

"On the barrelhead."

"Let's get the deed done, then. What room does Doctor Davidson typically use?"

"This first one here." He nodded and his coon hunting cap almost shook loose.

Kemp gestured for him to enter as a text came through with a ping on his phone. He glanced at the screen and let the clock reprieve loosen his attitude. Now, he had until five o'clock. He could definitely make that work. Delayne would understand his absence until then. She was used to the clinic's walk-ins, no doubt.

~

Though it had been over an hour since her last tear, Delayne's sinuses ached from her protracted crying spell earlier. The ICU hall provided a much more tranquil haven than the ER waiting room, as no one walked around bleeding in here. Maybe Kemp would appear at long last, sporting an injury of some type. That was the only excuse for making himself scarce that she would sanction. All other reasons were sure to land him neck-deep in hot water.

The more she thought about his absence, the more acerbic her attitude grew. *So much for facing life together.* That had been overly idyllic of her in a naïve sort of way. Her father might be dying for all he knew, but he hadn't found his way to the hospital yet. All he had to do was turn on his phone app and follow the map's directions. Eustace Springs had been founded on a grid system, so in a sense, all roads led to the hospital. Even that revelation made her angry.

Someone with scrubs on came down the hall, but diverted to the nurses' station before he got to her. Within minutes, they would be rolling her daddy out to surgery. Maybe she'd get a glimpse of him and could let him know she was there praying for him. She weaved her fingers together and bowed her head at the reminder. Prayer came with difficulty.

After she'd given some of her angst to the Lord, she looked up to find a patient being taken from her father's room. She rose and walked up beside the rolling bed. Under all the drip lines and monitor attachments, there lay her dad, looking pale and old. "Oh, Daddy. The doctor promises to fix you right up with this stent. Don't worry about anything." She squeezed his hand, taking care not to contact any of the tubes embedded in his wrist.

A tall figure bent down from the far corner of the bed. "That's right, Gaylord. And I've got the clinic covered, so don't you worry about that either. We'll stay as long as you need us."

They arrived at a double set of doors, and the intern gestured with a dismissive nod.

Her feet froze on the tile floor while the bed disappeared into the surgery area. The door flapped open once, and then shut for good. Tears welled up, but she fought them off. A hand soon cupped her elbow. She pulled away, a solar flare of self-pity launching in the moment.

Kemp stood in the hall, his palms open as though to protest being shirked off. His eyes held a question, though soft and concerned. "Sorry I'm so late, Delayne. A parade of clients kept showing up at the clinic. I stayed to help a few, but finally put a sign up."

"What if I needed you here with me more?"

He ran a hand through his hair. "I had to stay. What a privilege to do the work I'm trained for. Finally, in one afternoon, I get to *be* a veterinarian, not act like one."

When he reached for her arm, her patience snapped. She wheeled away. "I don't even know who you *are*." Pointed, she intended the words to hurt, and from the look in his eyes, they had hit the mark.

~

The hospital's chapel loomed beyond the double open doors. Kemp hoped to look at his situation in retrospect and have God's true light shine some wisdom on it for him. He'd sure managed to make a mess of things operating on auto-pilot. A shaft of golden sunlight beamed into the building over the altar up front like a beacon.

Delayne detoured around a grieving family in the back and headed down front. She stopped on the second row and slid onto the padded pew. When her elbow hooked the armrest, she seemed to claim her territory—alone.

He slid into the third row right behind her and planted his face in his palms. Glimmers of the busyness of the animal clinic flitted to mind, but he attempted to buff them out with more searching thoughts. People mattered, even to an animal doctor. Some people mattered more than others. He needed to reach out to mend the rift with Delayne, but had no earthly idea how. The only course of action would be to give it to the Lord.

Delayne slumped forward with a sigh, surrendered to prayer mode. Her hair covered her face and provided some personal privacy in the public place. The colored light of the cross-shaped window array played over the crown of her head like a divine presence.

Driven by an urge, Kemp couldn't settle for sitting still. In an instant, he strode to the step surrounding the altar. Under a golden shaft of light, he took to bent knee, his heart heavy. There, he begged for forgiveness in a whisper, asking for balance between his working and personal life. As he dug deeper to confess his single-minded aspirations for the clinic, his shoulders began to lighten of the burden. After a knee-aching eternity, he spoke his final words, locked the amen in place, and stood to return to his seat. Delayne was nowhere to be seen.

Chapter 14

Kemp didn't know this house, spacious though it was. The resident vet seemed to be a bit of a packrat, but his fondness for books balanced the excess. A tome appeared to be missing from his James Herriot collection. Perhaps he'd seen that book before at Lost Creek.

Delayne padded down the stairs, her hair in a lop-sided ponytail. The late nap must have been somewhat successful. She touched her fingertips to the corners of her eyes and blinked. "Hey there."

The room seemed to become lined with eggshells as he turned from the bookshelf. "So you got some rest?"

"Yeah. I really had to. My attitude needed…an adjustment. Thank God above that Daddy seemed so much better after surgery. What a major relief."

"You could see the improvement in his circulation, that's for sure." Something else needed improving, and he wouldn't let it go another second. He stepped closer and caught a wayward wisp of her hair, tucking it behind her ear. "I was wrong for leaving you alone for that long, Delayne. I can't imagine what you were going through. Please say you'll forgive me."

"I…overreacted. I had you by my side one minute, and then I didn't the next." She glanced up at him and her eyes held a far-away look.

"Had it been anywhere else but an animal clinic, I could have just walked away. I hope you believe that." Kemp wanted to touch her, but suddenly didn't know what to do with his hands. He stuffed them in his pockets for lack of any more promising destination.

She tucked her forearm against her ribs. "Oh, I know. That's why we're here, so the two of you can get together in a meeting of like minds." She leaned forward ever so slightly, cradling her midsection.

"Something's wrong, isn't it?" He took her by the shoulders and tried to read her expression. "Tell me what to do."

She rubbed her brow. "I don't remember eating anything at the hospital. Have we had dinner? My inner clock is all mixed up."

Relief flooded his senses. He could readily treat low blood sugar. "Okay, you're with me from here on out." He scooped her up and headed for the front door.

Delayne kicked up one foot. "But I'm not wearing any shoes."

"You won't need any where we're going. I spotted a Chinese carry-out joint on the edge of town when we came through earlier."

Her arms found their way around his neck. "Ooh, Chinese food. Yummy. I'd like a crab Rangoon with mine. Order me something with chicken, please." She flicked on the porch light.

He turned sideways to make it through the door with his precious load. On the front stoop, he paused to regard her delicate features up close. He knew he needed to do a better job of being a boyfriend, a much better job. "I hope this means you forgive me, little bird."

"Tweet-tweet," she replied, drawing up closer. "Forgiven and the offense forgotten."

He took the steps one at a time to keep from jarring her. Once he managed to open the car's passenger side door, he became reluctant to put her down. She made a tiny cooing noise against his neck that amplified his hesitation. He stooped to nestle her into the seat. A night breeze soon made her departure all the more dramatic. "Don't forget your seatbelt."

He walked around the car, trying to recall the route back into town. Everything would look different in the dark. He got in only to find her propped up on the console, looking soft-edged like a dream. Her eyes held anything but a far-away look now.

"Don't believe I've ever kissed you while I'm hungry, Doctor Junkowski."

"Well, that's certainly no way to live, now is it?" Already leaning in, he closed the gap that held her deprivation and allowed a deep taste of reconciliation to transpire. It had a mutual feeling to it, in no uncertain terms. He managed to start the car before they'd even separated.

She gave a throaty laugh. "Who seems to be in a hurry now?"

"Eating is much safer. Plus, I'm upping the crab Rangoon to two orders, so I can hardly afford any more delays." He slid the gearshift into reverse and veered into a wild turn-around.

"Go left out of the driveway. It takes exactly four minutes from here."

"Aha! So now you're lucid?" He turned as instructed and gave the gas pedal some pep.

"More like cashew chicken-focused," she replied. "I like your way of bringing a girl to her senses, I have to admit."

His ego swelled with the personal praise. "There's more where that came from."

"Which is why you'll be sleeping in Daddy's office at the clinic tonight."

He moaned for her benefit, having already spotted the overstuffed sofa in the office. "Now upping my crab Rangoon order to three."

"I want a cup of that red sauce, too." She ran a toying finger up his arm.

"Of course you do. I'll carry you up to the ordering counter to make sure we get everything your little heart desires." When her finger came close enough, he nipped at it.

She sat straight up. "Oh my. I forgot to let Strappy out and feed him."

"Done. He's asleep in his crate by the kitchen door. You need to relax."

She reclined in the seat. "I should chill out, because together we've got this covered."

"Now you're talking sensibly." He winked and targeted the city lights up ahead. An order of lo mein would balance out his order, and he'd feed it to her one slurped noodle at a time.

~

Delayne sat bent-legged with the clinic's calendar

of appointments on the coffee table in front of her. She waited until Kemp settled on the edge of the sofa behind her. The hot tea she had requested rattled to the tabletop on a mismatched saucer. Somewhere down the hall, a clock chimed midnight. "I thought we should take a look at this together."

"Good idea. He looks busy here, in stark contrast to my scheduled appointments."

"Can you free up your commitments so we can stay?"

"That shouldn't be a problem, at least until Friday. Becca comes in town with the doggie wash that day."

"Do you hide a key by any chance?" She took the cup and blew the steam away. A slight citrusy aroma wafted from the surface.

"No need. I've given her a spare key to the back door, just in case."

"Good thinking. I'm on contract with the natural resources department, so I'm done when my report is finished. I can get that accomplished next week or the week after, but my grant money runs out with the fiscal year. By July first, I'm history."

Kemp shifted forward and glanced at the calendar, then at her. "You're making me face a different sort of ledge, talking like that."

She gave his knee a friendly nudge with her shoulder. "Let's take this one week at a time. What did Daddy's doctor say? He'd be released by Wednesday at the latest, right?"

"Yes, but that doesn't mean he'll be ready to resume his clinic work. He'll have to build up his stamina first."

"Okay, look at these calendar entries. The next two

weeks are loaded with appointments. But afterwards, they tail off." She took a sip and looked up at him.

He traced the first five-day week with a finger, and then dropped it to the next series of squares. "People typically call and want to come in that week. He's booked himself as tight as possible for two weeks solid. We could always call and cancel—or reschedule for next month."

She shook her head. "Daddy wouldn't like that plan, I can tell you right up front. If we don't stay and help, he'll slip right back in there and do what he's always done—lose himself in his work."

"That's admirable—in a twisted way, I suppose. Listen, Delayne. This veterinary work is a complete adrenaline rush for me. Let's stay for the week. I'll conduct the clinic work, and you can take care of your father. Even better, come in to help me every chance you get. We can work together, especially until he's discharged from the hospital and back home."

"Plus, I can clean up around here and restock the fridge. I have Daddy's wallet and it's full of cash. Okay, we'll stay through the week. Now, try to think of everything we need to do back in Harrison to make this work."

"Guess I need a 'closed' sign up on my front door for possible walk-ins."

She cradled the warm cup against her chin. "Okay. Who can handle that for you? Think of someone nearby."

"Liv maybe? I have her number because she likes to relay messages to Becca for me. What should the sign say?"

"How about 'closed due to medical emergency' for

the front door sign? You could add a footnote that the doggie wash will still be in town on Friday. I think that covers it."

"Perfect. I'll text that to Liv tomorrow after breakfast. She can write it on a popcorn bag for all I care."

"Whoa. It sounds like someone is beginning to mellow out some."

Kemp scribbled a quick note on the margin of the calendar. "This is the opportunity of a lifetime for me. I only wish your father could be standing right next to me, telling me how to do each procedure the way he prefers. I've already found that the clients are most willing to steer me in the right direction as far as room choice goes."

"Ha! What creatures of habit you veterinarians are." She gave him a smug smile and took a sip of her cooling tea. A hint of honey made it exceptional.

"Well, you need the proper set of tools at your disposal, right? He has each room stocked differently, a real stroke of genius."

An idea came to her that seemed inspired. "Here's what I think. Daddy doesn't merely need a substitute. He needs a partner. Maybe that's the warning sign his heart gave him today. It wouldn't hurt him to slow down and share the load."

Kemp visibly shuddered. "What about Harrison? Are you thinking I should fold shop there? For the life of me, I haven't been able to drum up much business, even though the town's twice the size of Eustace Springs. It doesn't add up when you consider the demographics."

"It's the dollars that don't add up. The rural areas

surrounding the park are economically depressed. It's the dirt-poor Ozarks, remember? So even if folks have pets, they can't readily afford to have them treated."

"Maybe that's part of the explanation. Some of it is my inability to land any regular business, and forget repeat customers. I've been in business four months, and Strappy is the only animal coming back." He held his head in his hands, staring at the appointment-loaded calendar.

Delayne took a long sip. With the hour painfully late, she'd take a small step forward over a quagmire's delay at this point. Closing her eyes, she claimed a scripture that God would guide their steps in his ever-protective will. Eyes open, she nestled against Kemp's leg. "Let's watch for the good despite the pain. God is in control, though it looks like a knotted mess from where we sit."

"So let's commit to the week here. Gaylord will be home by Wednesday, and we can tweak the plan from there."

"Fair enough. I hereby commit along with you, Doctor Junkowski. And thank you in advance, on Daddy's behalf, for not letting his clinic shut down due to this…health hiccup."

"One more thing before I get banished to the clinic tonight." Kemp dropped his phone onto the calendar. His car keys soon followed.

Delayne rose onto the edge of the sofa cushion, wondering what kind of divesture she had witnessed. Too bleary to reason through it, she looked at Kemp askant.

He collected her hand and tucked it under his chin. "Father God, this isn't the friendly visit we anticipated." He paused when he saw her eyes flutter closed. When he cleared his throat, she opened them again. He gave her a wink of approval. "Most of all, Lord, we thank you that we were here when Gaylord needed help the most. By your orchestration, we managed the animal care while you managed his care. Now, he has a new lease on strong circulation that will serve him well for years to come. Help us make this transition work."

She squeezed his hand as a signal to add something more. "Teach us to number our days, Lord, and apply our hearts to wisdom. In the powerful name of Jesus Christ, amen."

"Now, can I talk you into letting me hold you for three minutes before I hit the sofa in there?" He nodded toward the clinic, but kept holding her hand.

"No," she replied, turning away. She twisted the lamp switch off so that only a nightlight from the kitchen area shone. "Not three minutes. No one counts the minutes. Only the days are numbered." She snuggled against him and fell into a giant hug.

~

Kemp stepped up into the main house from the clinic relatively on time. Since Gaylord's release that morning, he'd been all too aware that he might have an extra set of eyes surveying his work from time to time. Though he hadn't spotted the head of the house, Delayne had brought his lunch with a mention of restricted access. Maybe the four steps separating the structures proved too much for his host's weakened state.

Something from the kitchen smelled sumptuous as he entered the family room. He followed the aroma and found Delayne pulling a loaf of golden brown bread from the oven. Four chicken breasts sat in a sauce swimming with mushrooms and onions while a pot on the range top steamed. His mouth began to water.

Delayne saw him and nodded. "Oh good. You're running on time. I've made a special meal to welcome Daddy back home. This kicks off his restricted diet, so I'm hoping to prove that his taste buds don't have to die with the adjustment."

"I'm lucky to be a partaker of that demonstration. This looks great." He ran a finger across her back on the way to the sink to wash up.

"I may need some help getting Daddy out of his recliner." A pot lid vibrated in a puff of released steam.

"Count on it. I see you're back in your knee brace. Does that equate to excessive time on your feet today?" The water jetted from the faucet, so he tipped it back to a heavy trickle.

"More like too much housekeeping, but it's done now. Plus, I can rest after dinner. I plan to serve the food in ten minutes. Want to go give Daddy the day's rundown?"

"Now you're reading my mind." He dried his hands and grabbed the largest canister from the counter.

Her head jerked in his direction. "Where are you taking my flour?"

He removed the lid and showed her the stash of income he'd been stockpiling from the clinic since Saturday. "I'm taking this grain to the miller, so he can tell me how to grind it."

When two dimples appeared on her cheeks, he bent to cherish one with a kiss.

"Ten minutes, then I'll expect you both at the

table."

He whistled his cooperation and wandered to where the recovering patient rested in his recliner, staring out the front bay window. "Gaylord, how are you feeling this evening?" He perched on the edge of a club chair across from his mentor and held the canister in his lap.

"On the useful scale? Somewhere between a bump on a log and yesterday's newspaper. How did your clinic work go today?" He shifted the recliner back level with the floor.

"No time for daydreaming in there, that's for sure. Mr. Moore's Chihuahua lit into me before I spotted your warning code in the file. Fortunately, its bite didn't break the skin." He lifted his right hand to prove it.

He chuckled and gave him a sharp look. "So you figured out what 'star M' stands for, right?"

"Yeah, it means reach for the muzzle before you regret the encounter."

"Good one. You're learning, young man. Experience is the best teacher."

"Wish you could be in there with me, sir. Lots of second guessing happens throughout the day. I've been snooping through your cabinets trying to learn where supplies are stored, what you have in stock, and what you lack."

"Anything major in that last category? I can have DeeDee do some ordering for us."

"No sir. It's a well-run ship. Maybe by month's end, but no need to yet." He paused to review the rest of his day. A soft-spoken woman with caring eyes came to mind. "Oh, a lady named Nancy said she'd like to come visit you once you got comfortable being back home. I told her I'd relay the personal message."

"Well, socializing is the last thing on my mind right now." He harrumphed and leaned back in the chair.

"Sir, while we have a few minutes, I wanted to discuss the client payments with you." He pulled off the lid and tipped the canister toward him to display its contents. Wads of cash and several checks filled the storage container.

"My goodness. You have been busy in there, haven't you?"

"This includes Saturday's drop-ins after we'd supposedly closed. Those particular services got me in plenty of hot water with our cook, by the way."

Gaylord laughed. "How much did that cost you?"

"Chinese carry-out heavy with crab Rangoon. It had been a long day for Delayne. Did you know she used the AED to restart your heart?"

"Well, well. No, I didn't. I'll count that as one investment that truly paid off." His gaze returned to the window. "I didn't even know she'd be aware of the AED."

"Guess I can take some credit for training her on the device. I selected her from the crowd, the second time we met. She arrived on the front row, looking like a train wreck having already fallen off a ledge that morning surveying for birds. I delivered a bandage to her for the resultant bloody knee and saw a look in her eyes that made her hard to forget."

"She seems happy, even with the limp. A grumpy, middle-aged father ought to express some gratitude for that state of being. Your ability to take on the clinic work is over the top." His voice grew husky at the last admission.

"I've been sitting down in Harrison slowly dying while I wait for business to walk in. Then I come here and it's a textbook operation. Clients show up for scheduled appointments, and I get to doctor animals, the fulfillment of my training. Hopes and dreams get muddled up in stuff such as that, sir. By comparison, my operation isn't one, at least a successful one."

"Success takes time, but unfortunately trial and error doesn't pay the bills. Are you tied to a year's lease there?"

"No sir. It's a six months rental contract and I'm four months along. I'm questioning the renewal, actually. Especially if Delayne doesn't remain in Harrison come the first of July." His gaze dropped to his lap where the cash distracted him for a second.

"Then, give yourself those two months to make a level decision. Take all the cash from the work you're doing here and pay for that remaining rent. I'll have DeeDee make the bank run on Friday afternoon for all the checks."

"Sir, that's way too generous. It's mostly cash. Plus, I need to replace your supplies."

"We'll take a look at that once I'm able to get back to the clinic. I would have to hire help if you weren't here, so consider yourself on contract in general terms. If you're happy with the arrangement, I'm pleased to let you cover the work."

Kemp sat a bit taller as the weight of paying out his obligations rolled off his shoulders. "I'll have Delayne count this out, so we can have a record of each day's income."

"She knows the ledger system and has run deposits in for me in the past. However, all this domesticity is certainly a new venue." He waved a hand through the air and pointed to the kitchen. "You might take some credit for that, as I believe she's trying to impress you."

"Dinner's ready, Kemp," Delayne called from the dining room.

He stashed the canister and stood by the recliner. "Let me help you to the dinner table, sir. I'm under direct orders, so let's play along." He gave him a wink and grabbed an elbow to help him to his feet.

Gaylord grunted and managed an upright position. He took a couple of steps and paused. "I'll play along for now, as it takes less energy. That look in her eyes you mentioned earlier, I call it determination. Heaven help us if we get crosswise with that."

Kemp prompted him into another step, fully enjoying the collusion. He recognized the bare truth when it surfaced. That look of determination was part of Delayne's allure, but he planned to stay on the softer side of it, so help him God. "You know, sir, it's safer for her here anyway. Back in Harrison, there's danger lurking beyond every rock ledge. Plus, we've discovered an illegal chop shop running rampant right under our noses."

"Hmmm. You're whetting my appetite for drama, young man." He crossed into the dining room where dinner waited on the table. With limited assistance, he sat down to eat.

Delayne untied her apron and left it on the kitchen counter nearby. "No drama allowed, Daddy. Not during your recuperation." She blinked her eyes as though to put an end to it.

Kemp came around the table and pulled out her chair. "I'm taking credit for your newfound interest in domesticity." He gave a bow and gestured to the seat.

She tempered a little smile and settled into the chair. "If it makes you happy, go ahead."

Gaylord's eyes misted. "Thank you both for being here. I hardly deserve the assistance, even on my best day."

"We're here until you're back on your feet, sir. Please let me say grace tonight, as I'm feeling blessed the most." Kemp took Delayne's hand and gave her a tiny wink. Her cool fingers interlocked with his as his heart filled with gratitude for unmerited grace and a hot meal.

Chapter 15

Harrison had worn out its welcome in her conservative-but-accurate opinion. Delayne shifted away from the map and referred to her field notes to get the plotting accurate. Her two weeks in Eustace Springs had stolen fourteen days off the calendar. Plus, she'd gotten out of the canoe trip duty, as Timber had taken over her role in the stern. In fact, he'd become a regular visitor out at Lost Creek, an amicable progression she hadn't anticipated. A group project in the back of the lab dismissed, and several summer interns filed out.

She coded the next ruffed grouse sighting from her notes and placed the symbol on the master map, pressing it down an extra moment to make sure the adhesive held. Ross Connors walked past her station without a word. They hadn't spoken in weeks now. Why that didn't strike her as a perk, she couldn't say. Maybe she feared the pressure cooker was merely building up steam. She moved her fingertip beneath the next notation and assessed how to best delineate the sighting on the map.

A shadow cast over the corner of her notes. Manning cleared his throat. "Here is your letter of recommendation, as per your request." His voice stayed low to keep it private. "Guess I should say lucky sage grouse, but I really can't see you happily living in the desert."

"They call it gainful employment, though at my age, I really should try to settle into something more permanent." She shrugged her shoulders and accepted the envelope. After tucking it in the back of her field book, she gazed back up at him. "Any other deliveries I should know about?"

He looked around the lab. "My investigator thinks something may shift in the load by end of the month. That's pretty common in this type of criminal endeavor."

An unsettled feeling launched, pulling the skin on her arms taut. "Wow. That makes me want to vacate the premises at Lost Creek. What about Eva? Shouldn't we try to move her downriver?"

"They're well past middle river now, as Tim Price mentioned not using the launch at Pruitt anymore. You might be happy to hear I've pulled Tommy Lee Resnick off the lower river assignment. Price can stick it out and get the entire float accomplished with Eva. All the exercise is good for him anyway."

"The river looked high yesterday when I walked down to the bluffs."

"Yep. High levels now lead us into good water through midsummer. Maybe we can make it until

August before the river's too low to float."

"Sorry I won't be around to see that."

"You're not the only one who's sorry. Say, I'm breaking for lunch. Can I drop you by a certain animal clinic?" His face animated with the personal question.

"That's okay. Kemp is walking the puppy over in half an hour. I'll wait for them here, I guess." When he nodded and disappeared through the door, she focused on her notes again. Two more symbols joined the rest as her recording effort approached the last sighting.

"Don't think you're going to receive a commendation from me when you left like that for two weeks without any advance notification." Ross Connors snapped several papers through the air as though denying her something valuable.

She looked up and tried to harness her tongue from making the comeback he deserved. While she inhaled, a divine bestowment of patience must have alighted on her instead. "My father almost died alone at his clinic, Mr. Connors. I thank God a hundred times over that I was there and could help bring him around. Since I'm contract work for this department, not hourly, it becomes irrelevant when I finish my survey mapping, as long as it happens in June. Now, if you'll excuse me, I'll continue to work toward that end."

He started to walk away, but turned back in hesitation. "I hope your replacement aligns a bit better with the current staff than you have, Ms. Davidson. You might consider your long-term future before you start placing coworkers on official report for misdemeanor behavior contrived by your overactive imagination." He looked down his nose at her and left.

The word "misdemeanor" rang in her ears as her

blood pressure rocketed. Focused on the task at hand, she placed a symbol at the final grouse sighting and pressed the adhesive dot onto the master sheet. When she sat up to inspect the work under the light, she had rotated the symbol exactly sideways. In that direction, it resembled a bird's beak, not an arrow. "So much for not aligning," she said with a sigh. She spent the rest of her morning working toward perfection, a heightened state that no one around there would even appreciate.

~

"I can't shake the feeling that I'm dead in the water here." Kemp fixed his hands on his hips and walked into the tiny downtown park.

Delayne had to follow because Strappy took off after him like a spotty shadow. "Try to think of things you should be doing when business is slow. What about planning a special event to launch the groomer's service?"

"She should be the one planning that, not me. Every hour I sit there wondering how Gaylord is making out, and if he's keeping up with the schedule or not. How many appointments did we write in for him this week?"

"Twenty-four I think. Honestly, he'll be fine. I think he's asked Nancy to come work the front desk, so he has help."

"Let's qualify that. He has someone willing to answer the phone." Kemp fought getting riled up by wiping the back of his neck. He couldn't settle back into doing nothing after working full-time nonstop for two weeks. The downshift made him ache inside.

Delayne rubbed her palm along his forearm. "Don't punish yourself. You're building an honorable practice. It takes time to develop, that's all."

"I have two appointments tomorrow morning, back-to-back."

"See? That's great."

He walked further down the footpath. "Then there's a gaping hole for the remainder of the week."

"Remember, we're heading back up to Eustace Springs Friday after work. You two can catch up then."

A part of him that had been tensile and tractable now turned brittle and began to crack. "No, I'm driving back after that second appointment tomorrow. I'll call Gaylord tonight and tell him to expect me. I can be there before noon."

She spun with the dog's tug and faced away from him. "My mapping isn't finished, Kemp. For billing purposes, I have to be done by Friday, close of day. I'm out of options."

"You stay and I'll go. I can return for you Friday after the clinic closes, and we can spend the weekend up there like we'd planned. I think that works." He shoved off any guilt the change of plans tried to birth as he stood in the meager shade of a scrawny cedar sapling.

She went from being wide-eyed to blank-faced. "Maybe it works from your perspective. From mine, it seems lonely and…well…separated."

"What? You just said you *have* to finish up this week. With me gone, you'll have more time for work. You can even get started with your packing at Lost Creek."

Her chest heaved. "You live here. Your business is here. Plus, your doggie wash sidekick will be in town Friday. That's three reasons to stay put and wait for me."

Anguished at her refusal to come to reason, he headed out of the park at a brisk clip. When he passed the puppy, it naturally tried to heel. He halted, touched by the canine's gesture of loyalty. Looking back at her, he plowed past the sadness in her eyes and found the courage to ask. "So, who gets Strappy this week?"

She put her hand on her head as her expression turned sullen. "I do—the girl getting left behind to be lonesome."

"Fine. Stop by the clinic after work. We'll see you then." Knowing she couldn't keep the dog at headquarters, he held out his hand for the leash.

"Double fine." She smacked the handhold loop into his palm with a straightening of her spine. "I have to stop by the post office anyway, so I might as well get going." She stomped away which made the puppy yip.

Kemp fixed his gaze on the traffic to make the street crossing, his nerve endings jangled from the exchange. He glimpsed the clinic across the street, and it may as well have been a mortuary for all the emotion it stirred. The traffic light changed and he stepped down the curb, his little trainee right beside him. "If at first you don't succeed, fly, fly away." The words of surrender fluttered in the breeze much like the popcorn banner on a storefront down the way. A craving for caramel popcorn swept over him, so he detoured down the block to satiate the impulse. After all, he now had spare pocket change, like any normal working veterinarian would.

~

The rain that fell midafternoon suited Delayne perfectly. Tired of the map completion work, she had switched to finalizing her paper files. Her loyal field book would soon become part of this aggregate collection, a realization that dug under her craw a bit. She could take this data and easily turn it into a PhD at the University of Arizona, if she ended up there. The possibility didn't excite her in the least. She'd had a taste of real life here in Arkansas—with someone delightful to share it. Nothing else seemed to compare.

She shoved the field book into the recesses of the file cabinet only to retrieve it a split second later. At least she could copy the data and still have it available. Or better yet, she'd leave natural resources management the copied version and keep the original notations. She popped out of her chair and made her way up senior staff hall to access the copy machine.

When she crossed directly abreast of Ross Connors' office, his door flew open. He strode out wearing hiking boots and a scowl. For an instant, he regarded her much like he would have a squashed bug. Next, he turned toward the exit and left.

A second door opened and sliced her last nerve in half. In fact, she may have jumped a little. Her fingers turned to icicles, and the field book tumbled to the floor.

Dave Manning stooped and picked it up. "Hey, I was just coming to look for you. I'm doing the closing motor pool inspection. Can you come along for a few minutes—or are you busy?" He handed her the book with a questioning look.

"Sure. I'm not busy. I'm working…but I'm not busy." She shook her head like her brain might rattle inside.

He gestured toward the door and led the way back down the hall. "How's your father coming along?"

"Today is his first day flying solo back at work. Kemp is having some angst about leaving him to handle the load, so he wants to drive back up tomorrow once his schedule clears."

"That's commendable." A seasonal intern entered the building sipping from a gallon-sized cup from the local convenience store. Manning nodded at him and held the door for her.

Delayne walked out into the humid aftermath of the shower. The whole world smelled clean with the ozone rinse. She knew better than to think it could stay that way.

"I needed to get you outside where no one could overhear our conversation." Manning headed for the parking compound as another department vehicle returned from the day's assignment. "I checked into that sage grouse position at University of Arizona. Did you realize it held a federal grade level since it's a joint research project?"

She tucked her hair behind her ears. "Really? No, I guess I hadn't read all the fine print. I don't think that makes it a permanent position. It's a true two-year study."

"Right, but once you have a grade assigned, that makes it easier to lateral into another position when an opening gets listed. Easier for me, that is, to recruit you. I like working with those improved odds. By the way, tell me if you spot any missing vehicle parts."

"Will do. It sure would be easier for me to make this move to the desert if I knew it wouldn't last the duration. Say I go in to establish their transect array and get things set up for the undergraduate technicians to use during fall semester. Then I could pop out with the lateral move. Do you have any permanent job openings on the horizon?"

"Let's say I'm working on it. Connors is being followed right now. The investigator is sure something's going on this weekend. For that reason, I'm insisting that you pull out of Lost Creek by Wednesday." He tapped the trunk of a Ford sedan. "I can't risk you being out there when someone comes for those bumpers. And I know they will."

"Well, I could ask to stay at Kemp's place, since he'll be in Eustace Springs." The irony of that option stung immediately, as the object of her affections would seem close, yet still be far away. Her heart grew heavy. "What about Eva? Is any housing open at Pruitt for her?"

"No. She really needs to be on the lower river anyway, weather-permitting. Maybe she could start the campout portion of the float. Short of sending you with her, I'd have to team her with a male."

"I'm reluctant to narrow your options like that, but I'm not available this week. I have two solid days of office work that have absolute priority. Connors would love to dock my final paycheck, so I can't give him any justification. Sorry, chief."

The driver of the late-arriving vehicle slammed the door and walked toward them. Manning busied himself tightening the wing nuts on a license plate holder. Once the intern had made it to the rear entrance, he rose and looked her right in the eyes. "I'll send Eva camping with Tim Price for those last four days unless, in your judgment, that arrangement would not be trustworthy. Level with me, Ms. Davidson."

Why this felt like a test, she couldn't say, but

something about it seemed to possess a litmus touch of professional discernment. She thought about Timber and how Eagle Scout ready he always seemed. That demonstrated both a willingness to serve and a clean conscious. Physically, the young man was a massive mess, but at least he seemed ready to correct that negligence. Eva had even spoken about his weight loss in redeeming tones over the dinner table.

She blew out a long breath, unable to come up with any other suitable options. "At least Timber is capable of good decisions in the field. You'd want that working for you on a long float. Plus, I know Eva enjoys his company. I say pitch it to her, so she owns the final decision."

"She has to be out of Lost Creek by Wednesday night, as do you. Can you promise me that?" He pulled a moth out of a grill on a compact car that had backed into the space, a clear violation of protocol. With a snap of his fingers, he stepped over to check for a back bumper. He seemed relieved to find it intact. "Call me the little Dutch boy with his finger in the dike, because it feels like this whole thing is about to collapse."

She gave a hollow laugh. "If the flood is coming, we'd better be careful where we're standing when that dam breaks."

"With you holed up in that animal clinic, I'll sleep a whole lot easier. In the meantime, get that mapping done. As for my part, I'll pretend I never saw that field book, as long as I can find its contents in your files in some form."

"What field book?" she asked, tucking it behind her back. They had a pact, one that came with floods, deserts, and secretive birds that tried to live undetected lives. She'd spoil all of that with more intrepid field work, just like Manning hoped to spoil the chop shop heist. Nature could be more predictable than human nature, but only slightly more. The comparison lent her little comfort.

~

Kemp packed his duffel bag as the pup wrangled with an old shoe in the corner. He could feel the rumble of the dryer tumbling downstairs and made a mental note to listen for the buzzer to get the remainder of his clothes folded for the trip. After his last exchange with Delayne, he figured she'd be in and out for the dog, her bottom lip poked out at being left behind. That kind of emotional manipulation wouldn't work on him. He had a job to do.

He tossed the bag on his bed and headed for the door. When the puppy displayed its potbelly, he couldn't resist a quick rub. He would miss the little rascal, even with a steady parade of dog flesh coming through the clinic's door. Maybe he should insist on taking Strappy with him and appeal to her sense of fair play. What's more, her dad had demonstrated a fondness for the grand-pet, a point he would emphasize should the opportunity arise.

As he walked through the apartment, he noticed his lunch dishes still claiming the bottom of the kitchen sink. He'd tackle that now and not be hamstrung with the chore later. When he turned on the hot water, the line coughed, spat, and finally delivered potable water. A recurring irritant, he'd add that to a con list along with all the other inefficiencies that irked him about the clinic arrangement. The cons began to outnumber the pros, two to one.

With the dog's bowl left to rinse, the buzzer went off on the dryer. He tossed the dish on the drainer and turned to head downstairs. The puppy loped out, wanting to come with him. "Okay, buddy. We have to make this last night count, don't we?" He scooped it up to spare the usual time-consuming frolic down the stairwell. His feet beat a rhythm on the wood runners, the sound of a departing man.

He turned to the utility closet and stopped short, as someone had already salvaged the laundry from a destiny of wrinkles. Delayne stood there folding linens, wearing a dress of sheer rectangles that danced like scarves whenever she moved. Unprepared for such an exotic scene, attraction trapped him like a snare. He held the dog between them for a shield. "Hey. That was some rain this afternoon, right?"

She hummed a pleasant response and kept folding until the entire load sat in a tidy pile. "I brought dinner over. Hope you didn't have plans."

He glanced over her shoulder and spied two clamshell carry-outs that didn't give away their contents. That culinary intrigue stacked right beside the laundry. The quick exchange for the dog failed to transpire. When she stepped closer, Strappy gave a quick yelp.

Delayne ran a finger up and down the dog's snout. Then she took it and set it free on the floor. Her fingers found his shirt placard and began to explore that region next. "I wanted to say goodbye the right way, not by fits and starts." Her tone fell satiny in the private moment.

Kemp ducked his head and took an in-depth look at a fine work of female art. "I appreciate that. Once I had the notion to go back, that's all I could think about."

She touched a finger to her lip and transferred it to his. "I understand why you have to go." She came up on her tiptoes to close the distance between them. "That's what I came over to say. I understand." Her lips brushed his in a breathy touch-and-go. She went flat-footed again, but kept her eyes focused on him. "Want to eat now?"

"Maybe, in a minute." He slipped a hand around her waist and held her there. "I have to fix something first."

"Oh?" Her brow twitched ever so slightly.

"Yeah. You're pressure seems off again. It's better if you crank down and stay awhile." His whisper melted into a kiss, one he made sure went on longer than the wrinkle-proof cycle on the dryer. Instead of ending in a neat stack, he felt somewhat disheveled coming out of it.

Delayne stroked his beard. "I want half of your dinner…and you can have half of mine."

"Okay with me. Want to eat at the table upstairs?"

"Of course I do. Plus, I have an offer for housesitting that you'll find hard to refuse." She tugged at his hand and headed for the food.

Strappy attacked his shoelaces, reminding him of his next tactic. "Hey, I remembered how much your father seemed to like the little sparkplug here. Maybe you should reconsider and let me take him back with me."

She turned, the clamshells cradled in her arms. "I know. I should. Otherwise, those would be long days in the crate for Strappy while I finish my mapping. You were right to want him."

He almost recoiled from the ease of his success. He

wouldn't push his luck, but he seemed to have things going his way. This was much better than fits and starts and pouty little lips. To test her, he bent and gave her a kiss in passing. When she hummed with pleasure, it dug a tiny pit in his gut. He'd be giving this up to go spay and neuter the domestic animal kingdom of Eustace Springs. His justification balance quivered for the briefest second.

"Are you coming up?" She smiled and turned for the stairs. Strappy made a running leap and flew past the bottom step, a new favorite trick.

"Right behind you," he replied. After grabbing up the laundry stack, he reached for the small of her back to connect and made good on his promise. At least the night was young. That would give their farewell a chance for more proper pressure. He'd see to that.

~

Delayne flexed her hands to compound the conundrum. "I have to follow orders, even if it puts me out on the curb. To tell you the truth, I want to get out."

Kemp reached for her across the small table. "I understand that aversion to trouble. I think they call it common sense. Plus, you being here will be a load off Manning's mind. He's got enough to coordinate with an influx of federal agents."

"So I'll leave Lost Creek Wednesday morning for work and plan not to return. Are you good with me relocating here until the weekend?"

He rubbed his thumb across her knuckles. "One hundred percent good with it. Just bring your boxes and leave them in the clinic lobby if you need to unload some of it. I guess you'll be following me back to Eustace Springs in your own car Friday, since your job here will be over.”

A tiny gasp escaped her throat. She hadn’t thought that far ahead. By Monday, she’d be unemployed. If she moved back in with her father, she and Kemp would live miles apart. *How was that going to work?* When he clamped his fingers over hers, she gave him a feeble smile.

“I wish I could offer you a job. You’re overqualified as an assistant, but the perks can be pretty sensational around here.” His gaze grew warm as he stole possession of her hand.

With her palm flattened against his chest, she could feel the strength of his heartbeat. Her pulse seemed timed to match. Tonight she had him close by, but tomorrow he’d be gone. Their pending separation began to fill her with melancholy. “I’m going to miss you so much.”

Kemp stood and tugged her up with him. He reached for the half-wall by the kitchen and turned on a radio. A moody instrumental tune began to fill the apartment as the space between them evaporated. “We’re going to work this out,” he whispered, tucking her head under his chin. “Maybe I’ll work in Eustace Springs several days a week next month to help Gaylord.”

“So we can be together?” Her words seem to strain up her tightened throat.

“Yes, Layne. So we can still be together…and so I can work.” He raked his fingers over the crown of her head and held her closer as the music dropped to several thin notes and ended.

The break in broadcasting created an eerie silence that seemed to connote the death of something more. A sob broke from her lungs, and she trapped it against his chest. Finally, a lone violin poked the silence with a slow-paced refrain and she let the first tear roll.

Kemp's tall frame began to sway in rhythm to the music. He nosed the top of her ear. "This reminds me of that night in Hot Springs at the restaurant. We danced like this…and I seem to remember stealing a kiss. I sure didn't know what I was getting into." He reached for the rheostat on the wall and the dining room lamp overhead progressively dimmed.

With his arm pressed across her back, Delayne reflected back to that fateful night. She wiped her tears on his shirt pocket and sniffed. "I seem to remember that your car almost got the chop shop strip down right there on the mountain pass when I wanted to see the twinkling lights of Harrison from the overlook."

"Yeah, always something teetering on the ledge when I'm with you, little bird." He nuzzled her ear and gave it a kiss. "Always something." The violin took up the slow-advancing refrain, and he held her until her sobbing stopped.

Delayne surrendered the hopeless threat of tomorrow for the closeness of the moment. Her knees began to tremble, a ripple that had nothing to do with trepidation. A deeper current flowed beneath her as if being buoyed by fluid rock. She touched his neck with her fingertips to celebrate their togetherness.

He lifted her until her feet no longer met the floor. His cheek pressed hers. "I don't believe I've ever kissed you while you were crying." Then he made good on that first-time delivery, slower than the violin played and in the perfect key.

Her trembling turned back to tears, but this time joy

stirred the mix. When he lowered her to the floor again, she kicked off her shoes and put her feet on his, gaining height to remain in striking distance. It only took two steps for him to try out the new arrangement, a breathtaking maneuver of the bonding kind.

When the violin hushed, Kemp leaned back. His arms tightened into a smothering hug. "Stay safe while I'm gone, Layne…and love me when I come back."

"Ask for something more impossible." She settled the bridge of her nose into the cleft of his chin and tried to memorize how his silken beard felt against her skin.

Chapter 16

Delaynе stood by the Power Point image of her master map as the questions from her audience seemed to wane. Another stormy day to contend with, Manning had asked her to entertain the seasonal interns in a scientific forum Wednesday afternoon. Only Eva and Timber were missing from the ranks, having reported in hunkered down somewhere on the lower river to ride out the inclement weather. The impromptu presentation had taken all morning to prepare.

Ross Connors sat in the far seat on the front row, his ankles crossed in relative ease. He'd already asked several nit-picky questions on the study's methodology. Ingratiating even when silent, he sat plucking the eraser out of a mechanical pencil only to stuff it back in again.

Manning strode to the front of the room as the lights returned to full brightness. The washed-out Power Point image soon rested across his broad shoulders, the map symbols dancing with his every step. "I hope you can see, ladies and gentleman, what can be accomplished with focus, determination, and genuine scientific inquiry. The data at this thirty-year mark proves conclusively that the restocking efforts in the nineteen-eighties were worth their weight in gold for the species. I can tell you, we didn't have a hint of that back in the day. We only knew enough to open those transport crates and give it a try. The resiliency of nature took over from there."

Delayne stepped up beside him. "Don't forget the underlying message for our hands-on management of the ruffed grouse habitat," she added. "Extirpation doesn't have to be forever, so there's some forgiveness to be had with regard to nature. That's something mankind should hold precious, because it comes to us like a second chance—and we don't always get those."

"I've asked Miss Davidson to prepare a mapping exercise for your learning pleasure, but right now, let's take a fifteen minute break. I'd advise that no one leave the building—just some fatherly advice." When several protesting moans filled the room, he raised a hand up to quell the negative reaction. "In closing, let's thank Delayne Davidson for her thought-provoking presentation today."

The brief round of applause trailed off to random chatter as the occupants of the room stood to resume their hemmed-in lives. Delayne returned the remote control to the AV cart and went to shut down her computer. Halfway there, Connors intercepted her.

"That cluster pattern you mentioned sure repeated itself throughout the study area." He made an effort to glance up at the map still projected on the screen. "Almost predictably so."

Irked at his attempt to needle her with some inane nuance of deeper understanding, she started for the computer again. "It's not like plotting unknown constellations, Ross. The individual bird sightings form a cusp around the drumming logs. That's where the birds are active in the spring. Yes, that association might be considered predictable, in a sense, like fairy rings of mushrooms surrounding trees at their dripline."

"In that case, you might look back in hindsight and wish you had picked up on the indicators pointing out two distinct drumming logs just east of your first transect." He turned toward her and gloated. "The evidence is certainly there, like fingerprints on the edge of a photograph. Maybe we should consider that omission your legacy to the researchers yet to come. Indeed, you've set them up nicely with your incomplete work. Well done." He turned and left with a sneer.

Delayne stood in the empty room, searching her master map with a critical eye. Just before the turn-in for the logging road, a small cluster of sightings marked the possibility of a drumming log off-transect. Not even fifty yards upslope, the pattern repeated again. A tiny scorching sensation began to sear her temple. Surely she had missed something on that eastern slope beyond her lowermost boundary. She should have pressed the issue when Connors forced her into marginal habitat in the upper slopes.

With a shaky finger, she closed the file and then powered down the computer. Only two days remained in her tenure at Buffalo National River. Her files had been finalized, and she considered her work done. She closed her eyes and the telltale pattern flashed back onto her mind's eye. *What did it matter?* She should leave it right like that and give Ross Connors the satisfaction of guiding the next hapless soul right to the brink of discovery.

She closed the laptop and headed for the sanctuary of her cubicle, now starkly impersonalized because she'd already boxed up her things. She sat down and fished a six-pack of peanut butter crackers out of her backpack. When the first cracker alighted, it tasted like remixed cardboard.

The hands of an imaginary clock began to race in her mind as she contemplated her situation. She had two days, one more than she needed to document those probable drumming logs and add them to her findings. Even in the rain, she could locate scratch marks on the bark of downed tree trunks with one hand tied behind her back. She'd leave at dawn tomorrow, and then be back in the office by noon to map them. She wouldn't let on to Ross Connors. No, that would be his personal surprise when he opened her report and found the work fully updated. *Take that, Mr. Know-it-all.*

~

Kemp held his ground. "No way, I don't want you going up there."

"So you can go all the way to Eustace Springs for work, but I can't go to Ponca? Am I getting that right?" Delayne's insistent tone pierced the phone connection.

He knew to be frank, as she understood—and usually respected—directness. "Ordinarily, you could face-off with the testy bumblebee or wayward snake without thought of personal harm, but this is different." He lowered his voice. "Layne, please help me out here and play it safe. I'll be back in Harrison Friday before dark. We could go up together then if you want."

She exhaled into the phone. "I'm sorry I called you. I should have told Manning my plans instead. The fact is, I don't need his permission to check a vehicle out of the motor pool, and I don't need you babysitting me like a child. This matter addresses a professional oversight on my part, and I intend to rectify the situation tomorrow morning. Then, my field records will be complete—and my baseline work, flawless."

Kemp growled into the phone at her lack of cooperation. She seemed set to go no matter what. The chrome bumpers flashed to mind. He knew she had to steer clear of that stash. "Listen. I need your absolute promise on this—you will not go back to Lost Creek under any circumstance. Can you at least agree to that?"

"Okay, that part I can promise you. I told Manning I was out for good, so there's no need to go back. Does that help settle things from your high strung perspective?"

He gnashed his teeth until his jaw winced. Losing ground didn't seem to have any grace to it. "Say you'll call me the moment you're done. We're booked solid tomorrow morning, but I'll wear my phone on vibrate and promise to pick up your call. I need this excursion to be over with, so the shorter, the sweeter. Got it?"

"Piece of cake. Remember, this is what I do…field work. I have a reputation to uphold."

"Well, the funny thing about reputations is that they don't know how to sense danger." The night started to weigh heavy. He pinched the bridge of his nose.

"I promise to watch out for more than avian clues out there, just for you. I need to go find some food for a late dinner. You don't have anything in the fridge here."

"Welcome to the domain of a penniless, exasperated young veterinarian. Now, please be cautious tomorrow. Get in and get out."

"Ha! That was my exact game plan the fateful day I went up to Ponca and ran into you."

The humor of the coincidence missed him by a mile. He'd not end this in a begrudged compromise, though. He knew better than that, or he wouldn't have any peace. "Hey, your puppy is snoozing in your father's lap. Actually, I think they're both asleep. I'll leave the crate open in case Strappy wants to wander in. Be safe, Layne, and don't forget to call me."

"Goodnight, Kemp. Thanks for understanding."

The line went silent before he could even profess his affections for her. Too tired for regret, he slid behind the laptop screen to research induced labor in small canines. They had a tricky procedure scheduled at ten in the morning. He wanted to be in top form. At any rate, he'd save the magic four-letter word for her all-clear call tomorrow, a fitting reward.

Chapter 17

The pre-dawn sky banded in a blush of pink over the far ridge as Delayne pulled off the pavement at the entrance to the old logging road. She slid out with her field book, and then used great care not to slam the door shut. Working off-grid close to the road, she didn't want to scare away members of the resident grouse population. Any additional sightings today would come as extra feathers in her cap, but at a minimum, she'd get the coordinates on the two drumming logs. She checked her jeans pocket for the transect tags and felt the lump to confirm possession.

As she stepped into the forest, the emotional weight of paying her last visit struck out of nowhere. She'd gazed at this canopy line since early April and it had become something of a refuge for her. Even when matters had gotten testy back at headquarters, she'd always had the woods and rocky ledges to escape into. Within two days, she'd be giving up this sanctuary.

She referenced the old ruts to estimate where her

initial transect began, so she could stay east of that point with the new one. To follow strict methodology through the last day, she planned to mark both ends of the new transect with her permanent tags. A smooth-barked understory tree soon availed itself, so she tacked the anchor pin in place with the notebook. Thinking to note her starting time, she opened to the first blank page and began the final entry.

The forest floor gathered light from the break of day as she took her northwest bearing deep into the habitat. Hardwoods dominated the setting, and old logs littered the ground with frequency. Thorough, she stooped to check each log encountered. The anticipated drumming log lay more interior, but she wouldn't presume its location yet. Her next step set off a thunder of wing beat as a heavy bird took flight to her immediate left. She smiled and made notation of the grouse sighting, the small thrill delivering a jolt of satisfaction that she'd made the extra effort.

Time became of little consequence as the research plot absorbed her full attention. She mapped the first drumming log with a sense of certainty, as the cluster of sightings on the map taped into the front cover had virtually telegraphed it. Two more birds flew from groundcover at her approach and became part of the study. The second log fell in a remote depression beyond an exposed rim of rock. So popular with the courting males, all the bark had been scratched off along its center section. She guessed they'd been using this particular log for years.

Not to short-circuit the assessment process, she walked the full length of the transect until the woods began to clear for the adjoining homestead to the north.

When evergreens outnumbered the hardwoods in the ecotone, signs of bird use became scarce. She'd seen that same effect in the upper slopes, so she stopped to make a note of it. The edge effect cast pallor on her mood as well. The woods lost their magic at the artificial truncation of the canopy.

Delayne spied the barbed wire fence and decided to walk the last few steps to it as closure for the day's effort. She tucked the field book into the waistband of her jeans and extracted the final tag. The moment she touched the restricting wire, a metallic sound snapped the silence. She turned and looked right into the twin barrels of a cocked shotgun.

"Your word won't stand against mine that you're not trespassing in my field," the old woman said.

"Ma Resnick?" Disbelief swarmed Delayne's mind as she tried to make sense of the scene. "Don't you remember me? I bought one of your Dalmatian puppies this spring—the one with the cut cheek. I'm out here doing research for the park service this morning."

"No matter," she replied without a twitch of expression. "You're coming with me now."

"I don't think so. I have people waiting for me at headquarters." She backed away from the fence.

The homesteader lowered the business end of the shotgun. "Like I said, you're coming with me. Now you decide. Will that be with two feet or just one?" She squinted one eye and planted the stock on her shoulder.

A shiver slid down Delayne's back as the situation took on added gravity. Loss of a limb would spell a certain end to her fieldwork. The plucky old biddy was likely a keen shot, but she didn't intend to find out. "Fine, I'm coming with you. Lead the way."

"No, you lead the way. We're headed for that old barn back yonder. And walk so's I can see your hands at all times. If you try somethin'—well—the gun's already cocked." She gave a terse nod and the gun barrel shifted toward the pasture.

Delayne pressed the top strand of wire down and slung her right leg over. That precarious position somehow made Kemp come to mind. It looked like he wouldn't be getting his all-done call any time soon. When she tried to clear her left leg, her gimp knee caused her jeans to catch a barb and the denim tore. Off-balance, she tumbled into the overgrazed grass, a landing she hadn't anticipated. She struggled to her knees and grabbed at a lower wire. When she made contact, she hung the second transect tag on a barb hidden behind the fence post.

"Get yourself on up, missy. I've got folks waitin' on me, too." She hastened her with a kick of her boot.

Delayne rose, assessed the distant barn, and began to plot her next move.

~

Curse the bad luck. Kemp held the third stillborn terrier pup and placed it in the disposal tray with the others. It's seemingly perfect prenatal development tugged at his heart. Unwilling to open up the mother dog for immediate rectification of the problem, Gaylord continued to allow the birth canal delivery to snuff the life out of the newborns. The pet owner rocked back and forth in a chair nearby. The air in the exam room filled with tension.

"One more," Gaylord said. His hands worked with experience as the contraction process soon made another dark head appear. He handed the lifeless pup over to him with a guiltless glance and returned to care for the sedated mother.

Kemp began the same resuscitation massage that he'd given the others, working to clear extraneous membrane covering its muzzle. He compressed the pup's chest and worked each limb to try to stimulate the chest cavity into taking that first life-claiming gasp. Perhaps a few ounces larger than its littermates, he somehow didn't want to give up on this one. A begging prayer rode his next breath. With no further analysis, he clasped one hand to form a tube over its muzzle and forcibly blew air through its system. An instant later, the pup sneezed and all life precipitated from that point. Wiggles soon followed.

"Could you let me clean him up from here?" the owner asked.

Kemp nudged him with his elbow. "Yes, you can clean *her* up." He surrendered the puppy and reached for a hand towel to offer.

"Note the time," Gaylord said.

Kemp looked up and the wall clock read eleven-fifteen. He recorded the time on the terrier's file record and glanced at the door. "I think you've got an eleven o'clock still waiting in the other exam room, Doctor Davidson."

"You cover it, will you? I'm not quite finished here."

"Yes, sir. I'll do that." He turned to the sink and scrubbed under a hot blast of water. He pulled a paper towel from the dispenser and dried his hands on the way to another encounter of the animal kind. As he entered the door, he locked gazes with a woman who had hair the color of Delayne's. Sobered, he glanced at the clock again. She should have called by now. He patted his pocket to insure the phone was ready for her call. "What have you come in for today, ma'am?"

"I'm not sure, doctor. I can't seem to get Posey to eat anything lately." She shrugged her shoulders and put a carrying crate up on the table. From the grid panel on its door, two slanted blue eyes stared out like a dare.

Kemp immediately checked the file for any warning codes. The last thing he needed was a temperamental Siamese ready to shred his flesh. "Is she friendly?"

"Well, she likes Doctor Gaylord. Guess you'll have to take your chances."

He reached for the latex gloves as a compromise. Attitude bearing a full set of claws was a combination he respected. "Let's have a look then." He opened the cage. After crouching, the Siamese sprang out and landed three-quarters of the way up his lab coat. He extracted her from his chest with a tight grip. "She does seem light for her size."

"See? I told you."

It took all manner of forbearance for him not to roll his eyes. He could fix this with an advisement for canned food for three months, but would give the cat a frisk in case something was truly amiss. After his second thoracic palpitation, the creature arched, coughed, and belched out a sizeable hairball.

The owner shifted away from the disgusting sight. "Oh my."

"I think Posey will be feeling better now. I want you to switch her food to something with higher protein content. I'd go with canned food for the switch. Keep with it two servings a day for three months. We want it to be a total success, right?"

"Anything you say. You're the doctor."

He let his gaze cascade over her hair. My, how he appreciated full cooperation. "Thank you, Ms. Gutzman. You're helping redeem a tough morning." She made a little bow as he stuck the cat head-first back into the carrier. "Come back at the end of three months if the condition hasn't taken care of itself."

He led them out into the lobby and instead of finding the place cleared, three more clients now waited to be seen. His lunch break would shrink to nonexistent at this rate. Nancy shrugged her shoulders from behind the front desk and called the next client's name.

~

The hemp rope tying her hands may have been the least ancient item in the barn. Beyond the wooden hitch she'd been anchored to, Delayne inventoried half a dozen farm implements all in various stages of dilapidation, which matched the barn to a tee. The shelf above her head bore glass jars containing salvaged nails that seemed perpetually caught between assignments. A row of high-placed windows allowed sunlight to filter into the interior. She'd crawl out of one of those windows as soon as she busted a jar to get a jagged edge for cutting her constraining ties.

Her personal inventory still included her field book and her phone. Ma Resnick had been in too big of a hurry to take notice. Perhaps that had something to do with all the automotive front quarter panels squeezed into this rural storage space. By her count, there were one hundred and forty-seven fenders to report to Manning. That would be her second phone call. But first, she had to alleviate the wrist choke.

Her initial attempt to break a jar came with

laughable results. She lifted the hitch and tried again. This time, a jar spun on the shelf, teetered and fell—just beyond what her hiking boot could reach. She chose a pickle jar next and slapped against it with a rusty metal loop on the hitch. It broke in place, just above her brow line. On tiptoe, she mouthed a large piece and dropped it into her open palms. She wiped her mouth on her sleeve and began the sawing process. Cord by cord, the hemp gave way until she broke free.

She slipped her phone out and a message popped up with a faint ping. She glanced at the sender. It was Eva. Out of a sense of duty, she pulled up the text. The first line read *SOS*. Her heart nearly stopped beating at the second line as it contained only the word *Attacked.* As her mind raced with possibilities, her fingers found the number she needed. An act of God, the number soon rang.

"Manning here."

"Sir, I'm sorry to report trouble. Eva messaged me. She's been attacked and just texted me an SOS."

"Attacked? But I've already sent for them. The river went to flood stage with last night's rain. I made the call to pull them off the river as of nine o'clock this morning."

"Can I ask who you sent?" Delayne wiped over the sore skin creased by the hemp.

"Tommy Lee Resnick has the lower river. You know that."

"Sir, I don't think the Resnick family can be trusted. That's my second SOS. I've been tied up in a barn near the grouse survey area by a gun-toting Ma Resnick. This place is chock full of right front quarter panels, nearly a hundred-fifty at quick count."

The phone went silent for a few seconds. "Can you get out of there? The parts pick-up is underway today. We have surveillance trap set from Lost Creek on up. It's a big operation, Delayne. Get out and stay in the woods until I give you an all-clear."

"Yes, sir. I'm loose, so I'll climb out and make myself scarce."

"Good. We'll be up there within the hour."

She ended the call and searched for an exit route. The second window had a broken pane, so she aimed for it and started climbing.

~

Kemp had taken a late morning break that would likely count as lunch. He doubted the yogurt would stick to his ribs that long, but the afternoon would have to take care of itself. They had run close to schedule all morning, though it had taken two of them to accomplish it. Maybe Delayne had been right. He might be looking at a two-doctor operation. The thrill of being productive made him stand a bit taller.

As he passed through the lobby, he nodded to Nancy and angled to the front exam room. His phone vibrated, so he picked it up to make quick work of the call. He read Delayne's name on the screen and swiped to open the line. "Hey. You finally made it?"

"Okay. First, you were right to be cautious. Yes, I finished my work, but ran right into Ma Resnick .She toted a shotgun, a meet-up which lacked any cooperation. Then she proceeded to lock me up in a barn filled with car fenders."

The skin on his neck tightened. "Are you out now?"

"I'm loose and I've just climbed up the stack to shimmy through a broken-out window. I called

Manning. He claims the pick-up is happening today, so I'm to hide in the woods until he gives me the all-clear. The agents are set to make the bust at Lost Creek even as we speak."

An increasing discomfort began to run rampant through his chest. She seemed far from out of peril, too far for him to dismiss it. As he considered his options, a man appeared at the door holding a mangy mixed breed dog in a towel. He turned to the back counter to block the scene from his conscience, so he could deal with his danger-perched girlfriend. "I only have a few seconds here. How about keeping your phone on and let me know the moment you make it to the woods safely? Then I want you up by the UND transects, tucked into a crevice in the ledge for safety. Can you do that for me?"

"Roger that. Okay, I have to put the phone in my pocket to shimmy down now. I'll report back as soon as I'm across the perimeter fence."

"Fine. I'm going on stand-by." Kemp tapped the setting to speaker phone and turned toward the man who now stood beside the table. "Sorry sir, but I have to keep this call open. It's a matter of life or death." He slid the phone into his breast pocket.

"Sure. Go ahead."

"Tell me, when did this skin sloughing start here on your dog's shoulder?"

"Oh, first of the week, I guess." His eyes shifted to the problem area and then back up.

"From the looks of things, you're not talking about this Monday."

The man squirmed. "More like last week, I think, would be more when it started."

Kemp noted his reticence for the truth and reached

for the box containing latex gloves. He'd start the messy medicated rub and send the rest home with the owner. He took the prescription-strength treatment out of the overhead cabinet and heard Delayne grunt. Maybe she'd just made contact with terra firma again.

When he sat the bottle on the table, a struggle ensued over the phone. Delayne seemed to have fallen into a bit of a wrestling match. He paused and held a finger up to the client. Unsatisfied with the phone being in his pocket, he produced it and punched off the speaker option. Now tucked to his ear, he could hear her spitfire as she struggled against a great force. The impulse to bolt out of there struck him for the first time.

"Tell him to let me go," she said. "I mean it, Connors. I won't be held against my will."

Too far away to be audible, the reply seemed to lack any capitulation. Kemp stepped to the door without forethought. His mind raced. He needed a helicopter to transport him to her, but only had a tin box powered by pedaling squirrels. With a leaden pace, he approached the exam room where Gaylord worked.

A series of protests launched over the phone line as Delayne added a verbal attack to her thrashing against the enemy. Her voice soon became muffled and metallic clanks filled the line.

Kemp poked his head in through the door opening. "Sir, excuse the intrusion. It's Delayne. She's in trouble. I'll have to go back and help her."

Gaylord's brow shot into his hairline as their gazes locked. "Do whatever's necessary. Take my car if you want. It has more power, and the gas tank's full."

"Thanks, I will. Let me ask Nancy to cover the sulfur bath in room one."

"Oh, she'll love you for that." A hint of approval shined in his eyes.

Kemp returned to the reception area as Delayne screamed across the phone line.

"They're taking me to the Resnick farm." Her words came hurried. Several blows followed and the line went dead.

His lungs collapsing, Kemp shucked the lab coat and soon offered it to Nancy. "I have an emergency. You'll have to take room one. Bathe the affected area and send the bottle home with the pet owner." He dropped the coat, peeled off the gloves, and ran for the door. In strides, he had the automotive power necessary for the rescue. Now, he needed a miracle to shrink the distance between them. As he pulled out of the lot, a necessary link came to mind. He tugged out his phone and sent the call.

"Manning here," a low voice said.

"They have Delayne, sir. She managed to tell me they're taking her to the Resnick farm before the call got severed. I'm up in Eustace Springs at her dad's clinic, but I'm on my way. You're closer, so I need your help."

"You've got it. We sprung our trap here and can shift up there, pronto."

"Thank you. That's a relief. By the way, the fenders are being loaded from the barn west of the road. I could hear that going on in the background."

"Perfect, we'll catch them right in the act."

"Not to lessen your surprise, but Connors is there. Delayne mentioned him by name. I had asked her to keep her phone on until she reached safety…and it's a good thing I did."

"A good thing…and a bad thing." His tone seemed to cascade down a gravelly trail. "Tommy Lee reported in not fifteen minutes ago. He'd just dropped Eva and Tim off at headquarters, and then asked for the rest of the day off. I couldn't think of an official reason to deny the request. He could be pulling into Ponca within minutes. Gotta get moving. Goodbye."

Kemp hit the entrance ramp for the highway without slowing and the tires squealed in protest. By any count, he'd be the last one there. All he had was prayer at this point—and the performance ability to test the zero-to-sixty speed record, so he did.

Chapter 18

Delayne tugged against the line that bound her wrists, unable to loosen it. These thugs were more adept at the tactic than Ma Resnick, to her immediate misfortune. Over an hour had passed since they threw her inside what she now called the axle barn. She'd seen this dilapidated structure the day she bought Strappy. Now, she wondered if the big horse had cut his hoof in here. Granted, plenty of metal filled the place as car frames had been stacked shoulder high.

Something must have gone wrong with the parts heist up the line, as no one came for this particular cache. Maybe the quarter panels on the other side of the road had been a more immediate target. Where were the trucks hauling everything away? Too many loose ends dangled to let her be comfortable, not to mention the hemp line digging into her skin. She surveyed the inner walls again, searching for something to cut her bindings.

The barn door shook with a sharp blow. She sucked

in a breath and moved back on the hay bale where they'd stashed her. A second blow struck and the old door quivered top to bottom. The hasp must have given up the ghost because the door soon fell open a smidge. A liver-colored nose soon appeared and the crack widened enough for a rangy goat to fit through it. It headed for the hay bale and began to partake.

Delayne let out a breath, heartened to see pure daylight streaming into her prison. A second goat strolled in, with another following close behind. The hay bale became a veritable snack bar to a clientele whose ribs were showing. She slid from the top, stretching her tether to the wall as far as possible. A rattle at the door distracted her, and a horse hoof soon came into view. The horse pawed until the door obliged and fell open enough to allow the animal ingress. Now they were all present, one big happy family.

"Anybody want to nibble a rope appetizer?" She offered up her wrists and the big goat twitched its ears as if she had bothered their invasion. The horse strolled over and snatched a mouthful of hay off the bale. Delayne eyed the creature up and down, noticing its hoof had healed. An escape pod if she'd ever seen one, she only had to get mobile enough to use it.

~

Kemp pushed the RPMs as he gained altitude into the mountainous upper reaches of the park. As he passed the gate to Lost Creek and its campground, a convoy of unmarked white trucks had been halted up the access road. That justice seemed to be gaining momentum gave him a boost amid this landscape of isolated living that typically bred rebellion. If he could just extract Delayne from her predicament, he'd leave this god-forsaken country and not look back.

He pulled abreast of the grouse research site and found the woods crawling with federal agents on the round-up. When he spotted Dave Manning in the pasture where several police cars hovered, he decided to attempt a call. *Why isn't Delayne with him?* He punched the number up while the question haunted his thoughts.

"Manning here."

"I just got to Ponca. Do you have Delayne?"

"Uh, no. We've had our hands full across the road here. They had us four-to-one by numbers, but we had the element of surprise on our side. I had the pleasure of cold-cocking Ross Connors when he tried to escape. The bad news is I haven't seen Tommy Lee yet. So if you go over to the Resnick place, stay on high alert."

"Not *if* I go over, sir. I'm going there right now." He tucked the phone into his shirt pocket and wheeled the car around to make good on the promise.

~

Go figure. Hemp was inedible as an organic foodstuff. While the animals took rude turns at the hay bale, Delayne eyed a series of implements further down the wall. Maybe a curry comb would provide enough abrasion to fray the lines. She climbed back onto the bale and jerked at the hook fastening her to the barn's frame. Outstretched to her fullest extent, the curry comb now hung off the toe of her boot.

"Well, well, well. Now don't that look appetizing?" Tommy Lee Resnick approached the hay bale, the heated look of hormonal satiation on his face.

Delayne regarded him with contempt. "Don't get any ideas of touching me, Tommy Lee. You're in a heap of trouble already. I strongly suggest you don't add to it."

"What kind of trouble is that? I only took the afternoon off to help my Ma. Who'd ever guess I'd stumble onto a dainty damsel in my own barn?" He stepped closer and lifted a hand, inches away from touching her hair.

"Let's start the list of added charges with your attack on Eva. Somebody's going to answer to that, as she was on official business on the Buffalo."

He held his palms up defensively. "Not me. No, I like my women more…developed. Big boy's going to have to take the credit for that virgin-slaying."

The revelation blotted her rational thinking. "Do you mean Timber?"

Tommy Lee laughed and wiped his upper lip. "Haven't you noticed he's weak when it comes to temptation? All I had to do was provide the bottle of Wild Turkey, and he crashed his own train." He gave her a hungry look.

"What about protecting Eva's innocence?"

He shrugged his shoulders and stepped closer with a leer.

"Uncaring reprobate." With that epitaph, she doubled over, thrust her momentum forward, and planted the soles of both boots in a direct hit on his chest.

Tommy Lee reeled from the blow. The horse turned its head, but kept nibbling hay.

Delayne pulled at her tether, dying to be free. She wouldn't let him have his way, not with an ounce of fight left in her. And she had gallons…but no range of motion to unleash it.

~

Kemp parked the borrowed car out on the roadside to allow the powers-that-be access to raid the Resnick farm. That left him a considerable jog, which matched his pent-up steam. He ran until his lungs spit fire instead of air, but he could see the barn door open up ahead. That motivated him as he plotted his approach. Short on weaponry, his best attribute would have to be his God-given height. He would maximize its potential given the slightest provocation.

Delayne's protracted scream curdled the stagnant air surrounding the barnyard.

Unable to hold back, he hurdled through the barn door opening and broadsided Tommy Lee, lowering a shoulder into the man's back. They both tumbled onto the dusty floor and began to wrangle for supremacy. He ducked a fist aimed at his chin and clamped onto a slimy neck with a choking grip. Tommy Lee's eyes bulged with the reality that he was in for a battle.

Kemp jerked his opponent off the floor and wedged him against the hay bale. Delayne had retracted and now stood atop the bale, working feverishly on her own release. He took a kick in the shin that radiated pain up his leg, so he retaliated with a knee to the groin. Tommy Lee twisted like a fish on a line and momentarily broke out of his grip.

"Hold it right there, fellas," a woman yelled, her threat followed by the cock of a gun

Kemp shifted his weight to his toes as he crouched on the floor in recovery.

"No, you hold it," Delayne shouted. A rusted metal hook soon sliced through the air like a flattened cannonball. It struck the old woman on her collarbone, which sent the shotgun rattling into the dust. Spooked, the smallest goat escaped out of the barn door.

Kemp looked up in time to see Tommy Lee coming at him full bore. He locked his hands together and sprang at him from the crouch, unleashing his height advantage. Unblocked, the double uppercut landed on the attacker's Adam's apple.

Tommy Lee made a choking gag, dropped to his knees, and began gasping for air.

Delayne's arm soon wrapped around Kemp's back in solidarity, her booted foot denying further access to the gun.

A dark figure appeared in the doorway. "Federal agent—everybody freeze."

In seconds, Manning appeared. Several men began escorting Tommy Lee and his stunned mother into custody. He strode past them and surveyed the barn's contents. "It looks like we've recovered everything but the tires. Too bad."

Delayne broke into an inexplicable dash and faced off with Ma Resnick. After several animated exchanges, she returned to the barn. "Try the storm cellar for those tires, chief."

Kemp caught her by the arm and noticed her bloody wrists for the first time. "What did you say to make her cooperate?"

Delayne glanced up with a sheepish expression. "I mentioned that she might not like the citified food they served in prison."

He laughed and took her in his arms, lifting her out of the dust. "Oh, little bird. Whatever am I going to do with you?" One answer seemed most obvious, and he kissed her right under the horseshoe over the barn door.

The horse soon nudged his shoulder blade and a goat bleated for attention beside him. As he set her back down, he reconsidered the appeal of large animal calls. After all, a man could learn to appreciate a change of scenery now and then.

Epilogue

Of all the right moves Delayne had made, living in the desert would *not* be counted as one of them. Arriving in mid-July may have added to her misdirected collision with the hostile landscape, but the veritable lack of moisture made everything feel dried out. With a plan to exit this crispy landscape by Labor Day, September could not get here fast enough. She checked the door lock, glanced at the crated puppy, and started for the bedroom.

Kemp's last letter dated the third of August lay on the end table as she walked by. She'd already re-read it a thousand times. He'd managed to renegotiate his Harrison lease and still worked for her father two days a week. Though Gaylord was secretly underwriting his lease until the clinic could make a go of it operating solo, Kemp didn't need to know. She may have had something to do with that brainstorm, but he could claim the victory and lead the dual-location lifestyle that came with it. She had her own fussy birds to kick up.

She diverted through the kitchen for a drink of water. The desert seemed to wick moisture out of her from the moment she stepped outside. To date, she'd only seen one sage grouse—two if the mounted specimen in the lab counted. She glanced at the clock. It read eight-thirty. An early bedtime came listed with a host of other water conservation measures, all forfeitures to the sucking arrogance of the desert. *How did people survive like this?*

As she put the glass on the counter, a knock sounded at her door. She walked back through the living room, neatening her ponytail. A glance through the peephole revealed a caller with a purplish tongue. "Who is it?" she asked into the crack.

"Flower delivery," a man replied.

She unlocked the door and pulled it open. Crouched behind a bouquet of Japanese iris, Kemp rose with a dazzling smile. She clapped both hands over her mouth, but not before a tiny squeal announced her utter delight. She moved her hands when the questions started bubbling up. "What? Where? For how long?"

"Hey, it's been a long drive. Could I come in?"

She could only nod, but managed to take the flowers from him. Darting into the kitchen, she stuck the stems inside the glass and refilled it. The puppy barked, so she set it loose.

Kemp caught Strappy like a major league outfielder. "It was your father's idea, really, for me to come out and help drive you back home." He hugged the dog, looking road-weary, wrinkled, and totally amazing standing in her apartment.

"But I have three more weeks until the Harrison job

opens up. I have to stick it out here until Labor Day." She stepped up to him and tried to interpret his riddled expression.

"Okay. Labor Day weekend it is then." When the dog tried to lick his beard, Kemp put a gentle restraining hold on its muzzle.

"Well, you can't just hang out here in the meantime, can you?"

"Oh, that part. I took a visiting researcher's position with the Center for Sonoran Desert Studies. Did you know that Arizona has a desert tortoise care and husbandry program? They want to build a DNA database for the captive tortoise population, which I think is overdue. Don't you?" His question hung in the air until he gestured for her.

She stepped closer while words like "husbandry" and "overdue" circled back through her thought process. Her heart skittered in her chest. When she placed her hand in his, he folded his fingers around hers like sealing a trap.

"Mostly I came all this way to say it's not the same back home without you, Layne." His amber eyes spoke the rest as he bent to release the dog. "Will you take me to your magical desert and show me fanciful things like elephant trees and blue palms?"

Entranced by his gaze, she tried to formulate a reply. "You can't see the desert for the trees…I mean, you can't see the trees for the…Oh, mercy me."

He took both of her hands in his and shook his head. "No, no mercy for you this time." He dropped to one knee and looked back up at her, a fire burning in his eyes. "Delayne Davidson, I came all this way to ask you this one question. Will you marry me and explore a new survey site called 'togetherness' with me? I've discovered it's far too lonesome any other way."

She started trembling at the knees and soon knelt on the carpet to join him. Now she could look at him eye-to-eye. "Yet another bird takes wing that I didn't see underfoot. Truth be told, Kemp, I'm so lonesome my bones hurt."

He tipped his head toward her. "You still have to answer my question."

Her soaring spirit made holding back a smile impossible. "What's this? No drumming log imitation to capture my affections?"

He released her and began to beat his palms on the carpet. It made a sufficient rumble.

"Then my answer is yes, I'll marry you." Elated beyond belief, she fell into his arms and they tumbled onto the living room floor where he sealed the deal with a lingering kiss. Strappy added some canine affection to the scene, wiggling between them.

Once he released his grip, Kemp pecked her cheek and pushed away. "That leaves just one more task, like placing you on my survey map." He dug into his pocket and produced a tiny black box. When he worked the hinge, a faceted oval-shaped diamond graced the center of a platinum band. It twinkled with a hint of color, quite possibly the hue of forevermore.

Delayne tried to get her fingertips up to her eyes fast enough to block the tears, but he caught her left hand and made the fitting. She stared at the stone and allowed the tears to flow.

"It means eternal love, so you don't have to check the map legend for the corresponding symbol. "That should last forever," he teased with a touch to her chin.

She fell against his chest as his arms tightened around her. "Forever sounds almost long enough," she admitted. Then she placed her diamond-bearing hand across his heart to claim it for her own.

The End

ABOUT THE AUTHOR

of the landscape with sweet romance into authentic stories of man on the land. Immediately following her midyear graduation from the University of North Carolina Wilmington, the author took up residency at Steele Creek along the unspeakably beautiful Buffalo National River in the spring of 1983. Several portions of the perils from this fictional story arose from her varied experiences there working for the park service's natural resource management division out of Harrison, Arkansas. Though her experience lacked the handsome veterinarian, it did include an eleven-day canoe float down the majestic mint-colored river—frequently in the rain—mapping erosion banks along the way. She also became the first individual to observe the ruffed grouse population after its reintroduction from extirpation at the turn of the century. And the Dalmatian puppy was delightfully real, cheek scratch and all. Blaze returned to North Carolina with her afterwards, and got to live on an island chasing shorebirds to his heart's content.

Ms. Amos now writes inspirational fiction from her home in Wichita, Kansas. She ranches in the incomparable Flint Hills on the Amos family's fifth generation family farm with her aviation engineer husband and two strapping college-aged sons.

The author is a member of American Christian Fiction Writers national organization and faithfully serves as secretary in the South Central Kansas chapter. Find more on her website, including a ranching blog at http://cindymamos.wixsite.com/natureink. Like us on Facebook at https://www.facebook.com/NatureInkBooks

OTHER BOOKS BY CINDY M. AMOS

LANDSCAPES OF MERCY SERIES

Redeeming River Rancher

Saving Bicycle Man

Justifying Sound Strider

Sanctifying Ace Aerialist

Lifting Lock Runner

NATIONAL PARK ROMANCE COLLECTION

Everglades Entanglement

Mesa Verde Meltdown

50 STATES COLLECTION

Secondhand Flower Shop

www.ingramcontent.com/pod-product-compliance
Lightning Source LLC
Chambersburg PA
CBHW070445200726
48293CB00007B/2124